When a Rog̲ Woman
Rogues of Redmere Book Two
Samantha Holt

Chapter One

"How dare you?"

Lord Nathaniel Kingsley did not bother turning to face Patience. He saw from the corner of one eye the clenched fists pressed to hips while she glared at him. He thrust a fork into the hay and dropped it from one pile to another. A hiss of breath escaped her. Somehow, he kept his lips compressed.

"Well?" she demanded.

He gave her a sideways look, prodded the hay once more and slowly set the fork against the wall of the stable. The pungent scent of manure mingled with the fresher and more pleasant fragrance of fresh hay. The sheep that had been tucked comfortably in the stall seemed to take an interest once Nate turned and nudged against the metal gate holding her in place. Nate rolled his eyes and opened the gate to allow the sheep to trot out and stand by his side. The creature nudged him then stood faithfully at his feet like a loyal dog awaiting her owner's command.

Patience peered at this spectacle, one brow raised.

"What can I do for you, Patience?" Nate asked.

He brushed his hands down his breeches. With a break in the weather, he had taken the opportunity to ensure the sheep's lodgings were clean. The stable hands would do it normally but the sheep liked his company and, well, he had to admit the damned sheep was growing on him.

The sheep gave him another little nudge.

"What *is* it doing?" Patience blurted.

"She just wants attention. Ignore her."

"But...but she's just standing there, like...like a pet."

He gave a lopsided grin. "Well, she is. Sort of." The sheep had adopted him on one of their late-night trips to bring in the goods their smuggling ring had shipped from France. It had taken a strange sort of liking to him and insisted on following him everywhere. Only in the past few days had he persuaded the thing that coming into the manor house was not at all acceptable.

"You have a pet sheep?" She peered at him as though he had grown two heads.

He shrugged. "I suppose so." He began rolling down his sleeves.

Patience glanced at his bare arms. A hint of color rose on her cheeks. He tried not to grin.

The petite woman was hardly the sort he cared to make blush but seeing as she was on the warpath, he suspected keeping her on edge would not hurt.

Nate stared at her expectantly, arms folded. "I would urge you to make haste with your criticisms, Patience. I'm a busy man." He kept his lopsided grin in place as her fierce gaze raked his ruffled appearance. "You were about to get angry with me, I believe."

She lifted her chin. The sheep gave him another nudge. She glanced at the patient creature. "Does it have a name?"

"Not yet."

No one could quite agree on what a pet sheep should be called. Someone had suggested *Lamb Chop* which was not at all acceptable whilst others had wanted to call it something cute and fluffy. Nothing seemed quite appropriate.

Patience inhaled a long, audible breath. Patience, it seemed, did not live up to her name. It only made this all the more amusing, and what else did he live for in life but to be amused?

He saw her throat bob and she folded her arms over her chest—a chest that was quite ample for a petite woman. There was not much to be admired about Patience. She was small, but not in that sweet way that made a man want to bundle her up and protect her. Her shoulders were wide and her arms filled out the shirt she wore quite amply. She was, he supposed, what one would describe as robust. Of course, the breeches she wore did not help to make her look any more feminine.

"You should not have told your brother we were engaged."

He kept his expression placid and forced his gaze away from her breasts. "But we are."

"We certainly are not."

"We will be man and wife within the next few days. You might as well accept it."

She thrust up her chin and he took the opportunity to inch closer. Her countenance hardly wavered. Normally, he'd expect a little tremor. Not of fear, of course, but of something else. Women often trembled in his presence. Then they usually drew in a breath and color seeped across their chests and into their cheeks. Since the age of five and ten, that had been happening. But not this time. Not with Patience.

"I have no intention of being engaged or married to you, real or not," she declared. "I intend to travel to Falmouth alone. Why my brother saw fit to ask for your help, I do not know, but I am here to tell you that your assistance is not needed. You can stay here with your..." she waved a hand, "pet sheep, and leave this mission up to me."

He stepped closer. Patience had to lift her chin higher to maintain eye contact. Her brother, an agent for the crown, had asked him for help with his mission and Nate fully intended to fulfill that favor. After all, the man had helped them several times with keeping the customs men off the scent of their smuggling escapades. Nate and his brother along with two other men ran quite the operation, and it was bound to draw attention at times. When Jacob Grey had asked him to help and watch over his sister, he could hardly refuse.

"Ridiculous."

He arched an eyebrow. "Ridiculous?" The word had come from her so suddenly. She must have been musing their sudden connection, just as he had.

She pressed her lips together briefly. Jerking her head up, she kept her gaze steady. "Yes, ridiculous. this whole scenario is ridiculous. You should never have told your brother about the farce in which my brother intended you to take part and you should never have agreed to it in the first place."

"My brother needs a little shocking every now and then, and your brother asked a favor of me. How was I to refuse?"

"Quite easily." She rested her hands back upon her hips. "Here, I shall show you." She coughed and dropped her voice in an intimation of a man's. "Jacob, unfortunately I must decline. Your sister is quite up to performing this task on her own and I am not at all suited to it. I humbly apologize."

Nathaniel laughed. Patience did not look amused. Her brother, unbeknownst to her until yesterday, had asked him to help on a mission. It was known to only a few people that Jacob Grey worked for the crown. With Nate's experience of smuggling spies in and out of France alongside their smuggling escapades, he was one of the few. Alongside Jacob's sister, they were to track down a French woman who had information on Napoleon, and it meant pretending they were married. A harder task than he had first assumed, it seemed.

"You really think I am not suited to coming to Falmouth with you and protecting your honor?"

"Of course I do not. I'm not sure you know what honor is! The chances are, if anyone catches wind of us together, my honor shall be well and truly gone."

"It seems your brother does not think so."

"My brother hardly knows what he is doing. He must have struck his head after falling from that horse."

"He broke his leg, Patience, not his head."

"Could have fooled me."

Jacob was now bedridden after a fall and had been unable to fulfill his duties. With Patience's other brothers off at war, there was no one else to help him—apart from Nate.

"Face it, you are stuck with me. I shall not let you go to Falmouth alone and I certainly shall not pull out of a gentleman's agreement."

Patience snorted.

"You do not think me a gentleman?" He smiled.

"I would wager there are many women who do not."

"And you are one of them."

"I only know what I am told."

That did not surprise him. He could hardly claim to know Patience any more than she knew him. They saw each other at church occasionally and offered polite commentary on the occasional social event. Her father had been a well-respected retired General and, even after his death, his family attended most of the important events in the area. So Patience could not know him properly. But she would know of the gossip that followed. Gossip that was not always unfounded. Hell, why should he care what the old women of the village had to say about him? He gave no apologies for enjoying his life.

"Perhaps you have been told wrong," he reasoned.

"I have been told you are a rogue."

He chuckled. "And perhaps you have been told right. But rogue or not, I intend to see this through. We will go to Falmouth, I will pose as your husband, and we shall find this French woman."

"What do you know about finding French women?"

He bit back a laugh. "A lot, I can assure you."

Patience made a disgusted sound. "You must tell my brother you cannot do it. Surely you have other...things to do? Balls to attend? Animals to hunt or something?" She glanced at the sheep. "A sheep to shear?"

The sheep seemed to take a disliking to this and took two steps forward. Nathaniel clicked his tongue and the animal came back to his side.

"I find myself completely at your disposal." He took one final step closer—one that brought them almost toe to toe. Her nose lined up directly with his chest, forcing her to crane her neck. "Surely you have other things to do? Embroidery to finish? Piano practice perhaps?" He ran his gaze over her person and a tiny shudder wracked her at his perusal. "Dresses to try on?"

She thrust back her shoulders. It was likely not the first time someone had commented on her masculine clothing. Most of the locals simply considered her a little eccentric and turned a blind eye but there were still a few who made remarks about her attire. He paid little attention to the snide words. It was unusual indeed for a woman to wear men's clothing but in their small part of Cornwall, there were enough unusual characters to fill a lunatic asylum and generally Cornwallians rather treasured their oddities.

"As you can see, I have no need for dresses, and I certainly do not play piano or embroider."

"Imagine my surprise," he drawled.

"This is not about me, this is about you." She unfolded her arms and jabbed a finger in his chest.

Surprisingly hard.

"You must tell my brother you cannot do this and you must tell your brother we are not engaged before word spreads. I am certain you would be loath to find yourself married to me because you decided now was a fun time to tease your brother."

He rubbed the spot she had jabbed. "My brother already knows."

"He does?"

"Yes," Nate said with a deliberate slowness that sparked a fire in those amber eyes. "I told him that I was merely to pose as your husband for a short while in Falmouth, where no one would know me as the Earl of Redmere's brother and I would be under no obligation."

"You told him of the mission?"

"I told him enough. He knows I'm helping the crown. Believe me, if anyone can keep such a secret, it's my brother."

Patience nodded slowly.

If anyone was considered stalwart and honorable, it was his brother. The small collection of people who knew of the smuggling ring he had established a few years ago still thought of him as a good man. Those who did not know of it, thought him the best of men regardless. He was generous and kind to his tenants.

"You will not withdraw from this will you?"

"Absolutely not. I am a man of my word."

She glared at him for several moments but he refused to move or look away. The fierce look from the petite pale-haired girl would intimidate many a man.

He had to wonder where she had perfected it but he supposed growing up with four brothers had helped that. However, it would take more than a glare from a plain girl to force him into submission. He was rather looking forward to this mission. After all, it would give him a chance to escape the wedding preparations while his brother and fiancée arranged a great society wedding fit for an earl.

Patience huffed. "Very well, I shall speak with my brother. He will soon see the folly of his ways. You can expect word from him before long and you can go back to attending your sheep." She swiveled on her heel and stepped toward the entrance of the barn.

"Will *you* be the one bringing word?"

Patience paused and eyed him. "Not if I can help it. With any luck, we shall hardly need to hold a conversation again."

Wry amusement pulled at his lips. "I look forward to seeing you again, Patience."

"You won't see me again, my lord. Good day."

She strode away. If the ground had been hard, her boots would have made delightful stomping sounds but alas the previous day's rain had left it too wet.

Nate laughed.

Chapter Two

Patience huffed out a breath before she stepped into the house. Damn that man. Damn, damn, damn. This was her one chance to prove herself to her family and Nathaniel Kingsley was ruining it.

She shut the door behind herself and paused to listen to the tick of the Grandfather clock in the hallway. Hunting down Lord Nathaniel Kingsley had taken longer than she'd hoped and she was late for supper. Not that her mother would mind but with her brothers gone and Jacob laid up in bed, she felt it was her duty to continue the family tradition of always being rigidly on time.

Grimacing at the silent house that had once been so full of life before her brothers had grown and joined the war, she shucked off her muddy boots and made her way to the drawing room in search of her mother.

Pushing open the door to the drawing room, she found her mother in her usual corner, right by the window where the light was just right for painting. The scent of oil paints struck her instantly. Cordelia Grey had retained the honeyed fair color of her hair—a shade the same as Patience's though now peppered with a few streaks of white. Paint smudges covered her mother's cheeks and her fingers were tinged green, resembling long sprouting vegetables.

It was a sight Patience was used to. Her mother had painted for as long as she could remember, tucked up in the corner and creating scenery after scenery. It seemed at times that Mama preferred paints and oils to her family. She supposed it was her mother's way of dealing with an all-male family. Even with

Patience's presence, she would hardly claim to add anything feminine to their life.

She waited in the doorway, unwilling to disturb the long brush strokes and careful attention until the right moment. One wrong word or footstep and it would throw her mother off her stride and upset her. Her mother tilted her head, leaned into the painting and dabbed just so before turning her head toward her daughter.

"Are you late?"

Patience nodded.

"It doesn't matter you know, my dear. It is only the three of us after all, and Jacob will be staying in bed for the foreseeable future. You need not be so rule-bound."

She lowered the brush into a jar of water and swiped her hands down the apron covering her simple muslin gown. Built much like Patience, yet with a lot more height, her mother's face radiated a sort of warmth that always made Patience want to fling herself into her arms. But she was a grown woman and grown women did not want embraces from their mothers, particularly not when their brothers would tease them mercilessly.

"You're going to Falmouth I hear?"

Patience nodded. Alone, if she had anything to do with it. Though perhaps she would not mention that fact to her mother. She might not be the most traditional or even protective of mothers but she had a few standards and would not want scandal.

Patience could hardly care less about scandal. There was none to be had anyway. She was of good breeding but hardly nobility and no one in Falmouth would recognize her, she would be certain of that.

"Make sure you pack a good wardrobe," her mother said. "There may be opportunities to dine and dance."

"I hardly think I shall be dancing and enjoying myself, Mama. This is an important mission."

Her mother's smile took on a wistful air. "I know, my dear. I am sure you shall relish every moment. It is about time you had some adventure. But do be careful. Your escort is not the most gentlemanly of men."

"I hardly think I need concern myself with him."

As if Nathaniel Kingsley would be interested in her! A short, sturdy, barely pretty woman. Oh no, he would have far more exotic women in mind for his conquests. Not that it mattered as they would not spend time together. Patience would make sure of that. A quiet word with Jacob and all would be resolved.

"You would be surprised." Her mother stood and came close. Her hands came to Patience's cheeks, still cold from the paint and water.

"You are a fine young woman with much to offer," she said. "This is your first trip away from home without me or your brothers. I know you have been hungering for it but be warned, my dear, no matter how strong you are, life can send many surprises your way. Jacob tells me all will be well and that we must do our duty but it is hard for a mother to let go of her daughter."

"Mama," her voice caught a little.

Her mother dropped her hands from her face. "Well, would you look at me? What a silly fool. You are the bravest and boldest girl I know. Always have been, ever since you started walking. Always following your brothers and trying to prove yourself better."

"I will be fine, Mama. No one shall know. You can tell everyone I am visiting with cousins and I shall be back before you know it."

"Excellent. And on time, I should hope. Heaven forbid you be late." Her eyes twinkled with mirth as her mother knew all too well that Patience had quite the thing for timekeeping.

"I shall," Patience promised. She glanced at the mantle clock resting upon the large stone fireplace. "Is Jacob abed?"

"Indeed. I think he is enjoying the rest if I am honest." Her mother shook her head. "Who knew Jacob was even capable of rest?"

"I shall go speak with him. I must finalize the details of our plan."

Her mother eased herself back into the chair and picked up a brush and sighed. "All these plans. I shall never understand how I gave birth to these children who so adore plans."

Patience did not remain in the drawing room any longer. Once her mother had started the next brush stroke, there was no chance of having any further conversation. She backed quietly out of the room and mused her mother's candid affection. It seemed her going away had made her mother more appreciative of her. She smiled. Already life was getting better. Just wait until she returned with the information. All her brothers would be in awe of her and finally her eldest brother, Harry, could be proud of his annoying little sister.

Taking the steps two at a time, she reached her brother's room and knocked. She pushed open the door after hearing a muffled command to enter.

Her brother grinned when he spotted her glare. "Patience," he warned.

She strode over to his bedside and put hands to hips. Jacob was tucked carefully under several layers of blankets and propped up against the aged wooden headboard with several pillows. It was unusual to see her brother at home, let alone lying still but it seemed he could adjust to any situation, even being a patient, and was quite relishing all the attention.

"No," he said.

She jerked her gaze to his face. "What do you mean?"

"No. You are not going to Falmouth alone."

She opened her mouth and clamped it shut before drawing in a long breath through her nose. "But, Jacob, you cannot expect me to go with that man. He is a rogue!"

"Yes, which makes him perfect for the role."

She blinked at him several times. Six years her senior and the second oldest, Jacob had never had much time for her. He had been a good enough older brother but hardly bothered about playing with his irritating sister. However, she certainly never expected him to care so little about her safety and welfare.

Not that she really considered herself in trouble when it came to Nathaniel. But she had hoped to play on Jacob's protective side.

"Which role would that be? The one where he is to keep your sister safe? But who will protect me from him?"

Jacob laughed. "I am certain you can manage that yourself. I still recall you kneeing Michael Wetherby in the balls two Christmases ago."

"He tried to force a kiss on me. He deserved it."

"I am certain if you can handle Wetherby, you can handle Nate."

"But what does he know about working for British intelligence?"

"What do you know?" her brother pointed out.

"Plenty! I have been watching you all these years. I've studied everything that I can study."

"A few detective books does not make one an agent." His lips quirked with amusement.

Oh, how she hated that patronizing look. The only one who never bestowed it upon her was her mother. All the men in the family loved to smile at her like that. *Oh bless, little Patience is trying to be one of the big boys.*

"I can do this alone. I do not need help, particularly from a spoiled lord with no experience of anything other than chasing after petticoats."

Jacob pressed fingers to his brow. "Patience, he has more experience than you know. Trust me, he is perfect for this role. Besides, they need a man and a wife for this. That was the whole reason for me taking you. Now that I am unable to go, we must have a replacement, and fast. If we're to catch this woman, we must have you and Nate pose as husband and wife."

Patience made a disgusted sound. "I can do this alone."

"No."

"But—"

"No, Patience."

"Jacob, please."

He shook his head vigorously. "No. I trust Nate and you should too."

"Why should I trust a roguish lord who can only think with what is in his breeches?"

Jacob released a long breath. "Sometimes I think you would benefit from some ladylike company. You have clearly spent too much time in the company of men."

"Well that is not going to change anytime soon, is it, if you force me to go with Nathaniel Kingsley?"

"That is true but, alas, we have no choice. No one else can know of this mission so we must make do. You will go to Falmouth with Nate and that is that. Unless, of course, you would like me to find another woman or perhaps cancel the mission altogether?"

"Certainly not."

"There we have it then. You shall leave in two days and pose as husband and wife."

She pressed her teeth together until her jaw hurt.

"Do not look at me like that," he warned. "We have no choice."

"I suppose I had better go and pack then," she said tightly.

"Yes, you better had. And, Patience," he said as she went to the door, "pack a damned dress."

Patience huffed and stormed out of the room. Pack a dress, take a lord, pretend to be married. This mission was getting worse by the second.

Chapter Three

"There would have been many a heartbroken lass had you really been engaged," Drake said. His grin grew wicked. "I was looking forward to offering my comfort and condolences."

Nate shook his head and ignored his friend's jest. Instead he turned his attention to the ale in his hand. It would be his last for a while. He'd need a clear head for what was to come, especially if he was to keep that minx under control. If her own mother could not make her wear a dress, what chance did he have?

Either way, he was looking forward to the challenge. Smuggling was all well and good but they had only gone out once in the past month and all had been quiet. No excitement to be had. He was rather looking forward to the chance to indulge in some espionage and adventure.

Of course, Jacob Grey was aware of their illicit activities. Being a British agent had meant they had helped him before. He was one of the few residents of Penshallow who quite understood who was behind all the smuggling that took place in their small fishing village. Most thought Knight the face of it—the big, brooding, scarred hulk of a man opposite who spoke only when absolutely necessary.

At present, Knight's attention was on something near the bar. Nate flicked a glance over but could see nothing of interest. Only the usual overly drunk patrons gathered while Louisa, the innkeeper, worked her hardest to keep up with demand.

Other regulars littered the room, gathered around small tables. Some had cards in their hands while all had drinks. The Ship Inn was not the most savory of places but it was out of the way and the food was good. Not to mention Louisa was uncannily good at ensuring the customs men never came near the place. She had saved their skin many times and they repaid her help generously, ensuring she had a good supply of excellent French wine.

"You were a damned fool, signing up for this," Nate's brother said, thrusting a finger at him.

"What was I to do? You were off enjoying yourself with Hannah. Far too much it seems." His brother's gaze darkened and Nate immediately ceased any idea of talking of Red's fiancée.

Hannah was currently installed in lodgings in the village while they awaited the license for their marriage and to finalize all the details. His brother was, unbelievably, utterly in the love with the woman. It was not so much the woman he had fallen for that surprised Nate but that his brother had the ability to fall so heavily for her. Red had always been too busy to think of love, or even marriage.

Drake leaned in. The captain fixed Red with a slight smile on his lips. "Face it, Red. While you were distracted by petticoats, Nate held down the fort. I don't blame him for offering to help, after all, are we not in this to help the crown?"

"Since when are you so noble?" Red demanded.

"Since I have a pocket full of coin," Drake said smugly. "Things have been going uncommonly well of late. I don't see why Nate cannot help Jacob Grey and be back in time for our next outing."

"Uncommonly well?" Nate's brother lifted a brow. "After Knight's illness and the storm that near tore your ship in half, you were complaining of curses. Now you think things are going uncommonly well?"

Knight glowered. The giant of a man sat with his arms folded, a great scowl etched upon his face that in some lights looked as though it could be made of granite. Were it not for being friends with him, Nate would give him a wide berth. The man looked like trouble and, potentially, he was. No one really knew anything about him apart from the fact he was useful muscle and a damned hard worker. Though Nate suspected there was something more under that silent exterior. What that was, however, he was not sure.

"It was not an illness," Knight protested.

Drake laughed. "You vomited on my boots, Knight. What would you call it?"

Knight fell back into silent mode and glowered some more.

"Anyway," Nate said, taking back the conversation. "Aside from all of that, we have been doing well. The customs men have been chasing their tails and we've already sold on the last of our haul. As Drake says, we're meant to be helping the government, so why not agree to help?"

Red exhaled a lengthy, audible breath. "Do you know what this 'mission' is going to entail?"

"Jacob has given me most of the details. His sister—if she will ever deign to talk to me rather than shout—is fully informed. She was to go with Jacob and pose as his wife before he fell from his horse."

"So you are to play husband for a while?" Drake asked, his grin lewd. "Will you get all the advantages too?"

"Drake," Nate said, "if you met her, you wouldn't be bothered by the advantages. As it is, I'm fairly certain she hates me simply for breathing."

"Then you'll have to change that." Drake took a gulp from his ale and paused, his brow furrowed. "Jacob Grey. Is his sister not the one who always wears breeches?"

"And there you see why I would not even attempt to take advantage."

"Yes," the captain mused, "she would be tough to conquer. Great set of tits though."

"You are obsessed with tits," Red snapped.

"What man isn't?" Drake demanded. "You're still sore because I noticed Hannah's assets before you did."

Nate saw Red's fist clench at his side. The four of them had been friends for several years now and they all trusted Drake with his life. He was an excellent captain, even if he did get distracted by breasts far too often. However, when it came to Hannah, Red had no sense of humor whatsoever.

"I shall go to Falmouth tomorrow," Nate declared in an attempt to break the tension. "There we shall pose as this married couple and await the arrival of a French woman who it seems has pertinent information. Once we have the information, I'll return. I cannot imagine it shall take more than a week."

"And we have nothing of importance to do for another three," Drake pointed out.

Red nodded slowly. "We cannot go anywhere until the ship is fully mended anyway." His brother eyed him. "Just be careful, that's all I ask."

Nate rolled his eyes. There was only two years between them but because their mother had died whilst giving birth to Nate, Red had taken it upon himself to play the older brother role to a fault. The whole reason for Red setting up the smuggling ring had been so Nate could have a taste of adventure and help the war effort after he had discovered he needed glasses and could not get a commission. He was thoroughly aware of that, even if Red never said as much. But while he was appreciative of everything his brother had done, he needed Red to stop treating him like a little brother and recognize him as a grown man.

Potentially completing this mission successfully would prove as much. If drinking and tupping had not already shown Red, perhaps this was his chance to get out from under his brother's bloody shadow.

"When am I ever not careful?" Nate asked.

All the men around the table chuckled.

"What?"

Drake leaned in. "That time you decided to climb the cliffs and nearly drowned."

"I had no choice. The tide was coming in."

"What about the time you snuck into that woman's bedroom. What was she? A countess?" Red suggested.

"A marchioness," Nate corrected. "It was worth it."

Red groaned. "You were nearly killed by her husband."

Louisa approached with a fresh round of ales. She placed the tray down and grinned. "Don't forget the time he got steaming drunk and tried to challenge Knight to a fist fight."

"I would have gone easy on him," Knight grumbled.

Nate straightened. "I could have won."

"You were lucky the rest of us had clear heads," his brother pointed out.

"Well, I promise, dear brother, that I shall be the most cautious man there ever was. I shall find this French woman, with or without Patience Grey's help and get this information. And I shall do it without a whisper of trouble."

The men glanced at each other. Louisa set down the beers and tucked the tray under her arm. The fair-haired woman shook her head in amusement. "Sounds like you chaps need to make a wager."

"I wager he gets himself arrested," Drake said.

Red nodded. "Very well, I wager he falls for the French woman."

"Thank you for the confidence, brother," Nate said pointedly. "It means a lot."

"Louisa, do you wish to place a wager?" Drake queried.

She shook her head. "I never gamble."

The captain turned his attention to the behemoth watching silently. "What about you, Knight?"

"I wager"—he eyed Nate with the oddest look on his face—"Nate falls for the sister."

A laugh escaped Nate. "The woman in the breeches?"

Knight nodded.

Nate shook his head vigorously. "The woman hates me and I certainly have no interest in her. Big tits or not," he said with a look to Drake.

Knight shrugged. "Your family has a history of falling for the women they help. I think you will fall for her."

Shaking his head again, he chuckled. "Red might have a thing for stubborn women who need help but I certainly do not. Patience Grey is not the sort of woman a man falls easily for, trust me."

Chapter Four

The mail carriage to take them to Falmouth arrived half an hour late.

Patience nearly collapsed to the floor when it finally rolled up outside of Mrs. Whittaker's supply store.

Half an hour of standing with Nathaniel, of being far too aware of him nearby and of uncomfortable conversation.

At least from her side.

She doubted Nathaniel even knew what discomfort was. A man of wealth and breeding like himself would be used to being comfortable everywhere he went.

The moon shone brightly, reflecting off the silent harbor and highlighting the painted livery of the coach, declaring it belonging to the Royal Mail and emphasizing its stops that were carefully labelled on the side. No parcels were collected or swapped so they got on quickly and found the coach to be empty.

"I imagine the recent bad weather has put people off travelling," Nathaniel suggested as he settled himself.

Patience had chosen the seat opposite and to one side on purpose. That way she could keep her distance from him. From the amused smirk on his face, he understood her choice. However, she could not help wonder if sitting next him would not have been better. Yes, their bodies might have touched as the coach made its way across the rugged Cornwall terrain but at least she would not have to keep looking at him.

Not that she *had* to. After all, there was nearly a full moon out there she could eye. Or even the star speckled sky for her to watch go by. With such a clear night, she could even look at some of the scenery and admire the quaint cottages, their windows lit with the comforting glow of candles.

But, apparently, none of those things interested her more than her companion for the foreseeable future. Which was ridiculous. There was nothing interesting about him. Nathaniel Kingsley was a rake and a rogue. A man who took pleasure in the most sordid things in life and knew nothing of hardship. There was naught at all interesting about him.

The way his blue gaze skimmed over her and made her skin tingle was not interesting. The artful cut of his chestnut hair that left it just long enough to make one wonder if it was soft to touch was not at all intriguing. The wide set of his shoulders... No nothing to be seen there. Nor did she like the width of his chin or how his spectacles enhanced his blue eyes and made him look all the more intense and intelligent.

No. Nothing of interest there at all, and she would do well to remember that.

"If you and I are to work together, I think you need to be willing to speak with me, Patience."

Argh, she hated how reasonable he sounded. So much of her wanted to stamp her feet and throw a fit. *No, I do not wish to speak with you. No, I do not want you here. No, no, no, no, no.*

But that would not help her cause, would it? After all, she was meant to be proving herself and being a brattish young woman would do nothing for her.

"Very well," she said tightly. "Of what do you wish to speak?"

"This French woman, what do you know of her? I have had little time to get up to speed."

"Pauline Fourès was nothing more than a miller's daughter. She married a lieutenant in the French army and soon became rather popular with the men. It was not long before she caught Napoleon's attention but she would not be swayed. So he sent her husband on various missions, ensuring he had time with

Pauline until she finally consented to being his mistress. I believe they were together for two years."

"What changed? Why is she coming here?"

She could not help but smile. "Why else? She has been scorned."

"By Napoleon?"

Patience nodded. "And her husband. Napoleon lost interest after time apart while he campaigned in Spain. Her husband found out about the affair and it is said he has a terrible temper. She applied for divorce, stating she feared for her life."

"So she is escaping these men?"

"So to speak, but she wants revenge too."

"Ah. And the government wishes to use that to their advantage."

"Precisely."

"What information does she have and how do we know she has some?"

"Pauline has a second cousin living in Falmouth. Part of my brother's duties was to watch over those who were in some way related to Napoleon. They are obviously not his direct relations but Pauline wrote to her distant cousin, Francine, enough to warrant interest in her. The British intelligence has been intercepting and reading her letters for quite some time."

"That is how her departure to Cornwall came to their attention?"

Patience nodded. "She asked her cousin for help and a safe place to stay. But what was perfect for us—my brother and myself I mean—is that she has never actually met her cousin."

"And this is why you were to pose as a couple," Nathanial stated.

"And this is why my brother wants us to pose as a couple," she said, with a sigh. "Pauline is expecting to be met by her cousin and her cousin's husband."

She stole a quick glance out of the window to note their progress. They continued along the road that led over the hills, the moonlight frosting the tips of rocks and shrubs. Little else could be seen besides the occasional chimney from old and working mines and sometimes the milky light lit the ocean, revealing its expansive stretch toward the horizon.

"I could do this alone, you know." She turned back to him. "I have no need of your help."

"Not this again," he groaned. "And here I thought you would have resigned yourself to the fact that I am not leaving your side." He grinned. "Face it, Patience, you are stuck with me for better or for worse."

"It will definitely be for worse," she grumbled.

"Come now, I am not such terrible company."

"I would not know," she said haughtily.

"Do I detect a hint of longing?"

The moonlight caught his eyes at that precise moment, highlighting the twinkle of teasing in them. She gritted her teeth. "The only longing you detect is a longing to be alone."

"So you've never desired my company? Never been a little envious when I have say...danced with another woman?"

"Do not be ridiculous," she spluttered. "I loathe dancing."

He eyed her for a moment and she somehow kept her body still and fought the need to squirm. "What is it?" she finally snapped after too long under his observation.

"I don't believe you."

"That I loathe dancing?"

"No, that you do not wish to dance with me."

Patience rolled her eyes. "Your arrogance really does know no bounds. Is it that hard to believe that a woman might not wish to dance, and more specifically she might not wish to dance with you?"

He folded his arms and lounged back against the chair. The comforting rock and *clack, clack* of the wheels upon the road did nothing to help the moment. Patience tightened her jaw and eyed him back. What was it with this man? Did he simply enjoy riling her? Did he take pride in being wholly arrogant and rude?

"I have certainly never met a woman who does not wish to dance with me," he said after a time.

"Well, you have now."

He merely smirked.

"You have!" she insisted.

"If you say so."

Patience let out a near scream of frustration. "You are impossible."

"And you are not the easiest woman to deal with so I would say we are even."

Another almost inhumane sound of annoyance escaped her. She slumped back against the chair and turned her gaze pointedly out the window. There was no reasoning with him. He would never leave her be. Her only hope was she could escape his company once they reached Falmouth and do her own thing.

Nathaniel had apparently given up the fight for the time being and remained quiet. It was good. Yes. She liked the quiet. Far better than arguing with him, was it not? Even if there was something faintly stifling in the air. A sort of heat like a blanket closing upon her.

She stole a peek at him. He was staring at her. She turned away, warmth rising in her cheeks. No wonder she had felt odd. Anyone would while being stared at so obviously. She looked again, this time not so subtly. He still watched her.

"What is it?" she finally snapped.

"You know if we are to pose as husband and wife, you ought to show some affection for me."

"Not all husbands and wives are affectionate."

Her own parents, for example. Before her father's death, she had become aware there was not much love between them. She considered them like odd sort of friends. They had nothing in common and she never saw them touch each other, but they seemed to muddle along well enough as long as they both had their own space when they needed it.

"I always thought I would have some affection for my wife," he mused. "And I had hoped she would have some for me."

"Well, I am not your wife."

"For now."

She nearly choked on a breath. "What is that meant to mean?"

"Once we reach Falmouth, you shall be. In appearance at least." A smile curved his lips. "Though I suspect some will have a hard time believing it."

"Because a man like yourself would never marry a woman like me?"

"No, because a man like myself would not let you dress so. He would adorn you with the finest gowns and silks and..." He paused and Patience found herself awaiting the next sentence with baited breath. "And he would ensure your womanly assets were perfectly displayed."

Sucking in a sharp breath, she shook her head. "You, my lord, are truly scandalous. How dare you discuss my...my assets?"

He gave a shrug and chuckled. "They can hardly be avoided. After all, they are quite bountiful."

Patience snapped her head around and vowed to focus on the passing scenery once more. The shocking man did not deserve her attention. How dare he? How very dare he?

Yet...

Yet a tiny voice inside her told her she was pleased he had noticed that about her. It was so foolish it was almost laughable. She, who could not care one jot for appearing womanly and bountiful, liked that this arrogant lord had noticed her assets. She resisted the desire to press her head against the cool glass of the window. Could this get any worse?

Chapter Five

They arrived at Falmouth under the cover of dawn. The dusky light gave the town a romantic air though Nate knew the relatively large municipality could be a den for all sorts of goings on. The tightly winding streets where the old Tudor buildings nearly touched were a haven for the drunk, disorderly, and criminal. Nate came to Falmouth frequently enough, what with it being their nearest town and he had a sort of affection for it. It lacked the peaceful slowness that came along with living in a seaside village but he rather liked the anonymity of it. It certainly could not compare to London but it was a fine place to seek out his next adventure...or companion. Many attractive ladies attended the few social events and he had created many memories here.

The carriage slowed while it navigated the tight roads. Lamps were lit in a few windows and there were signs of people rising for the day, though only those who had a need to be up so early. A knocker-upper went by, a large stick in hand, useful for tapping on windows and rousing those who had no servants to ensure they were up for the day.

Of course, he would be creating new memories now. Ones that would involve Patience. His lips quirked when he eyed her mutinous pout and the way she kept her attention forcibly on what was happening outside. She had to have a crick in her neck by now, she had been staring out of the window for so long.

It didn't help that she made herself so easy to rile. Despite the unusual garments, there was something uptight about her, as though she was wearing the snuggest corset available. He wanted to dig under that loose shirt and jacket and pull at the strings to see what would happen. She was quite the riddle, this woman.

The carriage rounded a corner and the street widened. The houses grew taller and farther apart. Each cream house mirrored the next, with tall windows and a large black door central to every building, reached by four steps and a black railing. Boot scrapers sat patiently outside each one.

The mail coach came to a stop not far from the end of the road, next to a grocery store. There was a bustle of movement while packages and letters were unloaded so Nate rose and opened the door to step out. The fragrance of wood fires filled the air. He turned to offer a hand to Patience but she ignored it and stepped down. She gave a little stumble and he had to bite back a laugh while she glared at him.

"The house is just along here, I believe." She motioned down the road where the length of cream houses ended and branched out into two other roads. A few houses were scattered high upon the hills surrounding the town and Patience had pointed to one that sat at the top of a rather steep set of steps. At least they would not have any unexpected visitors, he supposed.

They made their way to the house, Patience hugging her large travel bag to her chest for fear of him doing something gentlemanly and offering to take it, he assumed. Well, he had little intention of offering right now. It would only lead to an argument and the journey and lack of sleep had left him too tired to fight.

"Here we are," Patience declared. "The Smiths' house."

Jacob had informed him that the cousins had been called away from town. He was not sure what British intelligence had done but they had somehow ensured they would not return until the French woman had been found. It was here that he and Patience would pose as this cousin and her husband, and hopefully make contact with Pauline. Then they would be able to persuade her to give over the information in return for protection from her husband and potentially Napoleon. The emperor would not be best pleased to find out his old mistress was giving away his secrets.

Of course, Nate would never treat a lover so poorly. All his conquests went away very happy women indeed.

The door to the house opened before they had even knocked. A short, slightly rounded woman answered and peered at them both. She was short, even compared to Patience, and that was saying something.

"Come on in," the woman said, glancing around. "Leave your luggage in the hall."

Nate did as he was told, placing his bags onto the black and white tiled floor. A white painted staircase, laid with a red patterned carpet rose upwards while a hallway reached past it, leading to a door at the end and one to the side of them. It was hardly comparable to his brother's house but the occupants would be wealthy enough and likely held at least another home elsewhere. A chandelier hung from the high ceiling but was unlit. Only two lamps provided the light in the room.

The woman hustled them into the room to the side which turned out to be the drawing room. Again, only two lamps were lit, just enough to cast a dim haze about the place. Several paintings of what Nate presumed to be local scenery hung on the walls, mingling with small, rounded portraits of elegant men and women. A fire burned in the stone fireplace, casting flickering fingers of light about the place.

"Forgive the poor welcome, my dears," the woman said. "I am under orders to keep your arrival quiet for the time being."

"We?" Nate asked.

"British intelligence." She smiled. "Mrs. Joyce Rowley at your service. I am to look after you for your stay as well as be of any help that I can. Mostly I shall be keeping you fed."

Nate peered at the short, wiry haired woman. Her thin lips and tightly pulled back black hair gave her a look of no nonsense but she had a friendly look in her eye and an open manner.

"A pleasure to meet you," Nate said.

"You are Lord Nathaniel Kingsley, and you are Miss Patience Grey?"

He nodded. "Indeed. At least for now."

"Have you heard any word of Pauline?" Patience demanded.

Joyce gave an appreciative smile. Apparently, she was keen to set to work too. "Nothing yet. Mr. and Mrs. Smith left two days ago. We are blessed with them being out of the town. As long as we keep you hidden from sight, no one shall notice that the Smiths returned as different people. Our hope is that Mrs. Fourès shall try to make contact before long and visit the house."

"And hopefully bring us that information," Patience finished.

"What exactly is the information?" Nate asked the woman.

Joyce gave a smile. "I am afraid I do not know. I am merely a lowly housekeeper."

"For British intelligence," Nate muttered.

"I have cooked and cleaned for many important men and women," Joyce said with pride. "However, I am rarely privy to the important information. There are several files awaiting you in the study that were sent down prior to your arrival."

"And you wouldn't know what was in them?"

Joyce's smile turned mischievous. "Not at all."

Nate tried not to grin. The housekeeper might claim ignorance but he knew if he were in her position, he would have snuck through the files himself.

Patience nodded. "We had better look through those now."

"Already? Would you not like some refreshment first?" Joyce asked.

Nate was about to agree that he would not mind a coffee at all but Patience shook her head. "No thank you. Let us look at those files and then we shall have a drink and something to eat, if you please."

"All business," Nate murmured.

Patience shot him a glare. "Is the study through here?" she asked, motioning to the door at the end of the hallway.

"Through there and to your left. I shall ready some drinks for you and bring them in. I think Lord Nathaniel could do with something."

Nate gave the housekeeper a grateful smile.

Nate dutifully followed Patience through the house to the study. The fire in the room was unlit. A stack of papers awaited them on a mahogany desk. Two book cases covered one wall, the spines old and dusty. Most looked as though they had never been touched.

Nate waited while Patience leafed through the information. He would read it himself shortly, once he had consumed a coffee. He strolled about the room and picked up a book. A cloud of dust consumed him and he let out a sneeze that would not be held back.

Patience glared at him.

"I hardly sneezed on purpose," he declared.

She waved a bit of paper at him. "Mrs. Fourès played Napoleon well it seems. She ensured he wanted her desperately before giving in to being his mistress. It seems, though, there may have been some affection there, particularly as she was not happy in her marriage. When he lost interest, it likely hurt her."

"And she lost her husband too," Nate added.

"Some might say that was a blessing, including Pauline by the looks of it. If she was right, he might have been a danger to her. But our Madame Pauline was not happy with simply escaping. From the letters they've copied here it's clear she wants revenge and to secure her safety. What better way than to hold important information in enemy territory?"

"Why does she not simply give it over?" Nate asked.

Patience shook her head. "She probably still loves him. She is probably using the information to ensure she is left alone. We are dealing with an intelligent woman by all accounts. It says here, in her letter, if anyone threatens her, she shall reveal the names of several French spies as well as information on Napoleon's next movements."

He rubbed a hand across his jaw. "All of which could be a huge help to the war effort."

"We need to ensure she comes out of hiding and we need to be the ones who gain her trust."

"Sounds simple enough." Nate strode over to the fireplace and eyed the miniatures in gilded frames of various family members. "We wait, you pretend to be her trusted cousin, and if needs be, we reveal our hand and ensure she gives over the information."

"When you get to my age, Lord Nathaniel," Joyce said as she entered the room with a tray of coffee and biscuits, "you realize nothing is ever simple."

Nate glanced at Patience and found he had to agree with the housekeeper. There would be nothing simple about being in Patience's company. Nothing at all.

Chapter Six

The incessant tick of a nearby clock rattled through Patience's brain. *Tick, tick, tick, you can't sleep,* it told her. She tossed to one side, aware of the strange sheets sliding against her skin. The mattress gave a creak and she heard a carriage rolling by outside, the driver whistling a far-too happy tune for what had to be the extremely early hours of the morning.

Patience huffed. "I give up," she muttered.

There was no sleep to be had. Her mind was insisting on running over every little incident from when her brother had first announced she was to pretend to be Nathaniel's wife to now. She could not stop thinking about that confrontation in the barn and how roguish and...well, attractive Nathaniel had looked in shirt and breeches. And then there was that sheep. Who had a pet sheep, honestly? But there was something about his fondness for the creature that appealed to her. After all, demonstrating a kindness to animals was hardly an unwanted trait.

Then there had been their conversation in the carriage. If one could call it a conversation.

Very well, for the most part it had been an argument.

But within that argument had been information her brain had kept hold of. For example, he had talked of displaying her figure. She should be disgusted by such bawdy talk. She *was* disgusted. However, that irritating little voice that could not be tamed was secretly pleased.

She blew out a breath. Pleased! She of all people. She did not give a fig about being seen as a woman or a man noticing her figure. Heck, if she did, she would not be wandering around, inviting ridicule by wearing what she deemed as more comfortable clothes. It was all well and good looking pretty and inviting admiration but how could a woman do anything in such restrictive clothing? No, she would not be wearing a dress unless it was absolutely necessary and it had nothing to do with wishing to show off her figure to Nathaniel.

Not that she really had much of one. Her arms were too thick, so were her thighs. She did not even have much of a defined waist. Sturdy, her mother called her. Enough people had definitely called her masculine, even with her rather large breasts. If it was not for them, no one would consider her womanly at all, especially Nathaniel.

Patience threw back the covers and sucked in a breath of air. The night was cool but the embers from the fire in her room continued to give off a little warmth. All her tossing and turning, however, had made her hot and aggravated anyway, and she had developed quite a thirst. She would have to make her way through the strange house to find a drink if she was to ever get some sleep.

The wooden floor on the soles of her feet gave instant relief. She inched open the thick curtains to let in a little light so she could navigate her way around the unknown room. Even though they had plenty of time after lunch, their discussion had revolved around the French woman and their future plans. All of which seemed far too vague and frustrating to her. But she had yet to properly look around the property.

Smaller than her own house but still grand and elegant, it contained four bedrooms plus rooms for the servants. Joyce was upstairs to keep up the pretense. She said she preferred the simpler rooms anyway.

Easing open the door, she stepped out, keeping her door ajar so she could return easily if her hands were full. She might as well see if there was some food to be had too. Her stomach grumbled a little after being unable to finish her dinner. Joyce had cooked a fine supper but eating opposite Nathaniel left a lot to be desired.

Not that he had terrible manners or anything of the like, but it was disconcerting eating opposite a man of his looks and demeanor.

Patience crept downstairs, regretting that she had not stopped to grab a candle from her bedside. Each darkly shadowed corner offered some new danger. A table to knock into or a vase or an umbrella holder. Her smallest toe seemed to find and connect with every one of them, leaving her cursing aloud as she made her way through the house to the kitchen.

She found the stone steps that led down to the room and hissed. The stone might as well have been made from ice blocks. She should have slung something on over the man's shirt she habitually wore to bed.

A hand to the railing, she ascended the steps with caution until she reached the bottom. The stone slabs of the kitchen floor were no warmer or kinder but at least she could no longer complain of being hot. Perhaps once she returned to bed the strange sheets would feel warm and comforting.

The kitchen windows were high in the ceiling. They would just peek out at the bottom of the building to let in what light there was to be had. Had it not been for a lone candle, resting upon the long wooden table in the center of the room, she would likely be stumbling around blind. She paused and listened for a moment. Was someone else up? They had to be to have left a lit candle, surely? Yet she could not see nor hear anyone. Perhaps they had gone to bed and left the candle burning. It was down to a mere slither of wax, after all.

She picked up the candleholder by its curved handle and shrugged. At least she would no longer be stumbling around and striking everything with her poor, abused toe.

"That's mine," came a deep voice.

Patience screamed and whirled. Or perhaps she whirled and screamed. Either way, she reacted so quickly she hardly had time to register the face attached to the voice before she flung the candle and its metal holder at the intruder. There was a hiss of pain from the man and a loud curse. Patience whipped around the table only for her toe to strike one of the table legs. She yelped and nearly toppled to the floor.

She would have too, had it not been for the grip of a man's hand upon her arm. She screeched again and brought back her fist. He grabbed it before she could do anything with it.

"Damn it, Patience, how many other men do you think are in this house?"

She struggled again, even while her brain began to register the reality of who was in the now pitch-dark room with her. He gripped her tighter, hauling her close so that she was pressed against his body. While it might have taken her a while to understand this was Nathaniel, it did not take her long to recognize the lack of fabric between them. When her chest struck his, she was certain but a scrap separated them. Her hand came to his chest in an attempt to steady herself and she discovered she was right. He was either entirely naked or only wearing some briefs or breeches.

Patience closed her eyes. "Please do not be naked, please do not be naked," she whispered.

Nathaniel chuckled. "I am not."

She opened her eyes again and sighed. "What were you doing? I could have hurt you." Now that her eyes had adjusted to the dark, she could make out his profile and the light from the upper windows caught in his eyes.

"Too late."

"But—"

"Hot candle wax is not the most pleasant of greetings."

"You should not have been sneaking around. I had to defend myself."

"I was not sneaking. *You* were sneaking."

"I most certainly was not."

"What else would you call tiptoeing around barefoot?"

"I was merely looking for a drink and trying not to wake everyone."

She saw that arrogant smile slip across his lips and settle comfortably in place. "What a coincidence, so was I. Struggling to sleep?"

"Yes," she confessed. "I am seldom away from home. And if I do travel, it is to stay with my cousins in Devon. I'm unused to strange surroundings."

"Well, I am quite used to sleeping in other beds—"

"I bet you are," she muttered.

He ignored her comment. "But it never gets easier."

The revelation startled her, no matter how small. How was it this man—who likely did spend many a night in the strange beds of his female companions—could not settle at night in anywhere other than his own bed? She would have expected him to feel so secure, so comfortable wherever he was that he would have no concerns about falling asleep. Did he too toss and turn at night and worry over matters of which he could have no control? The idea of Lord Nathaniel Kingsley acting at all human had her speechless.

"Shall we see if we can find another candle?" he suggested. "Just in case you forget who I am again and decide to punch me once more."

"I did not punch you."

"You were going to." He released her and only then did she realize she had become accustomed to his body close to hers and the way the strength and warmth of him made her feel comforted.

Comforted! Preposterous. This was a man who would take advantage of any situation. Why, if she were some beautiful widow with an elegant figure, he would not be releasing her so quickly. She knew enough of his reputation to understand that much.

He gripped her hand, though, to guide her around the kitchen as they played a sort of blind hide and seek.

"Here, candles, candles, candles," she whispered, unable to resist.

"I have my suspicions they do not come when called." She heard the rattle of something as he fumbled in one of the drawers.

"It was worth a try."

Not thinking about her hand tucked in his was also worth a try.

She did try. And failed. Over and over until he finally declared he had found some candles. He released her hand to light them and recovered the discarded candle holder, then used it to light a few scattered about the kitchen. It was not enough to light the whole room but they created an amber glow that ensured neither of them would be smacking into kitchen tables or throwing punches at other household guests.

She bent to inspect her still throbbing toe then straightened. "I do not suppose—"

Patience froze when she considered his eyes. One brow was raised, his body was stiff and unmoving. The only part of him that did move was his gaze, which darted down to her feet, up her legs, over her chest before starting the movement again.

Fiery heat flared in her cheeks when she finally realized quite why he was acting so bizarrely. Her attire was of course not the norm for a woman of her age and breeding. Or, well, any woman really. The fact was she found chemises too constricting. The fabric always tangled around her legs and the high necks made her feel as though she was being strangled. After deciding her brothers' shirts looked much better, her mother had given up and started giving her all her brothers' old clothes. At least she was not wandering around naked, was her mother's conclusion.

Patience coughed but Nathaniel did not get the hint. She tried again, and he eventually snapped his gaze up to her face.

"You wear men's shirts at night?"

She nodded.

"*Men's* shirts?"

"As you can see."

He shook his head and chuckled to himself. "Of course you do."

Chapter Seven

"I hasten to add," Patience said, far too matter-of-factly for a woman who was practically naked, "that this is not the first time you have seen me in a man's shirt."

"Nor will it be the last, I'm sure," Nate drawled. "But I have never seen you in *only* a man's shirt."

And what a sight to behold it was.

He'd been aware that Patience had some redeeming qualities. Two to be precise. The way the cotton carefully caressed her breasts and drew his attention had him wondering if he'd been spending too much time with the breast-obsessed Drake. He was normally an arse man.

Not when it came to Patience it seemed. But it was not only her breasts that drew his attention. Her legs were surprisingly long for a short woman. Though not slender, they were strong and capable-looking. Just the sort of legs perfect for when the woman was on t—

"Stop staring," she hissed.

"You're staring too."

He had only just noticed. After all, he'd been far too busy leering at the unexpected delights that had been hiding under those baggy masculine clothes. Why did she hide herself? No doubt she considered herself free, unconstrained by womanly garments, but he suspected it was more to do with disguising herself than anything, whether she was aware of that or not.

But she was staring, and she certainly was not hiding it. Her gaze ran over him like that of a ravenous wolf. She should have licked her lips to finish off the picture. As it was, her top teeth came down to bite upon her plump bottom lip. He near groaned.

"I am not staring," she said, her voice a raspy whisper.

She was. Still. Nate lifted his chin a tad and straightened his shoulders. He was no stranger to female admiration but, he had to confess, Patience admiring him did more for his pride than one hundred looks from society ladies. Given that she loathed the very air he breathed, it was quite an achievement.

Nate took a step closer. A little experiment just to see. She did not move, instead seeming to sway slightly into him.

"You stubbed your toe?" he asked, keeping his voice low.

Oh, she was far too much fun to toy with. And, of course, that was what it was. A game. What else could life be for a second son? No responsibilities, no heirs to bear, no future set forth for him. Had he been able to join the military perhaps it would have been different but he would not dwell on that fact. He would only play so far, of course. They had a mission to do and while he enjoyed teasing her, he did not touch virgins. Unless they begged and there was little chance of recourse, naturally. But he doubted Patience would ever beg.

"Pardon?" she asked, her gaze remaining latched upon his chest.

"You stubbed your toe?"

She nodded, her teeth still digging into that lip delightfully and making him want to pull it between his own teeth and suck at it until it was even more plump and red.

Nate put his hands to her waist and heard that satisfying inhalation of surprise. She stiffened but he had little trouble lifting the small woman onto the table.

"Which foot?"

She peered at him as if he was speaking in a foreign language.

"*Parlez vous Anglais?* Which foot?"

"The left."

He took her foot in his hand and eyed the toe in the candlelight.

"What are you—"

Apparently, the fight had returned. She tried to wriggle her foot away from him but he kept his grip tight around her ankle.

"Nathaniel, put me down."

Alas, the effect of his bare chest had not lasted as long as he had hoped. Had she continued to be so malleable it would have been easy to have this mission completed swiftly. He would have to try harder next time. He smirked at the idea of walking around naked simply to ensure he did not get completely dominated by this woman.

"It is not funny," she hissed.

"I was not laughing at you," he assured her. "Now keep still and let me see your toe. You might have broken it."

"It is fine," she insisted, giving one last wriggle before letting him manipulate her toes.

Delicate feet, slender ankles, and muscled calves meant he had a hard time concentrating on her toes. The shadows between her legs beckoned. He was willing to bet there were no men's briefs on under that shirt. Christ, if he was not careful, any control he thought he had would be gone. He gritted his teeth and eyed her foot.

"Seems fine."

"I told you it was." She kicked out at him then jerked her foot back before hoping off the table. "You, on the other hand..."

"Me?"

She put a finger to his chest and tore off a lump of wax that had covered his person during her attack.

"Ouch."

"Baby," she teased.

He eyed his chest to see the now solid wax had left a red mark. It would be gone by morning but that did not mean it felt particularly pleasant to have it torn off. She picked at another wax splodge.

"You would make a terrible nurse."

"I have little intention of nursing you." She viciously, and deliberately, tore the biggest piece of wax from his arm.

"Good God, woman. I think you took half of my hair with it."

"Probably." Her smile was far too self-satisfied.

"Witch."

"My mother says witches were unique and powerful women, who were merely misunderstood."

"Perhaps I did not mean it as an insult."

She gave a half-smile. "I doubt that."

"You have me pegged as quite ungentlemanly, do you not?"

An eyebrow arched. He had to admit, he quite liked the way the candlelight brushed across her smooth skin. His fingers twitched with an urge to stroke her cheek then perhaps trace a line down to her neck, then in between—

"Not ungentlemanly—and I could hardly complain if you were, as I am not exactly a lady—but you did tell your brother we were engaged without my consent. Hardly the behavior of a gallant man."

"My brother is too wrapped up in his own engagement to worry about my fictional one. And I disagree with you not being a lady."

She blinked at him several times. "You would be the first then." She flicked another bit of wax off his shoulder. "And I am fairly certain your brother worries about you regardless of his own marital state."

Nate shrugged. "Perhaps. But I do not need him to. I'm sure you can well understand how frustrating it can be having a brother watching your every move. You have three after all."

She shook her head. "They're all too busy to watch my every move or even pay attention to me. I would be grateful for a brother like yours, Nathaniel."

He heard the wistfulness in her voice. It seemed odd to him that her brothers were not more protective. If he had a younger sister, he'd likely not let her out of his sight, particularly with men like himself around. No matter how contradictory that was.

"Red is a good man. Better than I to be sure."

"A hard example to follow."

"Precisely." He grinned. "Which is why I carve my own path."

"Spoken like a man."

He let his grin expand. "In case you had not noticed, little one, I *am* a man."

"It is just so very easy for men to speak of their own paths. There are no such paths for women to follow." She folded her arms. "And I have a name."

"Yes but *little one* suits you so well."

"I am not a child."

"*Meine kleine fräulein*, then."

"No!"

"*Ma petite mademoiselle?*"

"Certainly not. What is your obsession with other languages?"

He shrugged. "Most women find it charming."

"Not me."

"Little one it is then." He glanced around the kitchen and found the pitcher of lemonade he had discovered in the larder whilst looking for a drink. "Did you come here for food? Or drink?"

Patience huffed. There was no arguing with him. "Both ideally. I found myself quite hungry after dinner. The travelling must have whetted my appetite."

Nate tried not to consider any appetites that were being whetted at present. He poured a lemonade and set down the platter of cheese he had found on the table. They both sat, taking a chair next to one another. If Nate thought hard about it, he'd find he liked the quiet companionship that had settled over them but he really did not wish to be thinking of something dull like companionship for the moment.

"Can you cook?" she asked, taking a chunk of cheese and taking a bit from it.

"Do I look like I can?"

"No."

"And you?"

"Not really. I baked a few cakes with the cook when I was younger but I think my father complained about the smell."

He scowled. "The smell of cakes?"

Patience gave a little laugh. "Yes, cakes of all things. I think he was not happy unless he could smell gunpowder or oil all the time."

"I imagine it's a hard adjustment no longer living the military life."

She nodded. "Oh yes. I was too young to remember of course but my brother Harry says he missed the army sorely."

"I had pictured the same for myself once, but of course," he motioned to his glasses, "these do not much help."

"I cannot imagine you enjoying the discipline of the army."

"Well, it was not so much the discipline I wanted but the adventure. There's much to be said for one to have a goal in mind, so the military seemed perfect. You are forever being given a new goal."

"Yes, that always appealed to me too."

He peered at her. "You envy your father and brothers for going off to war?"

"Why would I not? They are afforded the ultimate opportunity to protect their country. What can I do? Stay at home and raise morale? I think we have enough finer ladies than I to do such things."

"You forget the main risk of war, which is, well, dying. I do not think your family would be too happy about that."

"My family live and breathe the military. With the exception of my mother. She tends to do her own thing and ignore it all when she can. I think sometimes it's too much for her to deal with—all her sons off fighting battles and such. But my father and his father and even my uncles have done nothing but serve."

"And here you are, unable to follow in their footsteps."

"I am not so foolish to romanticize war, Nathaniel." She took a long sip of lemonade and he found himself distracted by the arch of her neck while she drank. "But it always makes me wish I was doing *something*."

"Now you are."

"Yes, as are you. But I still do not need your help, regardless of what you say."

Nathaniel gave a dramatic sigh. "And here I thought we were finally coming to an understanding."

She peered at him with an odd sort of smile. "I do not think we will ever understand each other, Nathaniel."

"Nate," he corrected.

"Nate," she said, albeit with a little uncertainty. "You are a wealthy second son with all the advantages the world can offer you. I am a supposedly gently bred woman whose only goal in life is to find a husband. You can imagine how many offers I have had so far."

He did not protest. Patience would have a reasonable dowry but she had no connections and the mere fact she wore men's clothes would put off a potential husband in an instant.

"Not that I ever want any, anyway. I would rather die alone than marry."

"Come now, we are not all so terrible."

She lifted her chin. "I have yet to meet a man who can convince me otherwise."

Nate wondered if he should consider that a challenge but he strongly suspected he was not the man to do so. He could tell her that he was not simply sitting around and twiddling his thumbs while men died at war but, firstly, it was too risky to tell anyone else about their smuggling antics, and, secondly, he could not quite decide if such information would raise him up in her eyes or lower him, considering her probably rule-bound military background. Better to remain quiet and let her think whatever she wanted of him. In the meantime, he would try to keep his attention from her breasts and those strong legs and focus on the mission at hand.

He glanced at her cleavage.

He would. Definitely.

Chapter Eight

"You shall wear a hole in the carpet."

Patience glowered at Nate. It was well enough for him—he was used to sitting around with nothing to occupy him. Not her, though. If she was not out riding or shooting or going to town, she was cleaning the house or helping Mama organize her paints. She had never spent so long with so little to do.

"She should have arrived by now. She must know."

"Madame Pauline may well be delayed."

She shook her head vigorously and peered out of the window of the drawing room. People came and went below them, like little figurines darting between the buildings of the town. But there was no sign of this French woman.

"We cannot sit around forever. What if she never arrives? What if she's heard that Mr. and Mrs. Smith are gone? If she is a smart woman, she shall know we are not them."

"*If* she is a smart woman."

"You think she is not?"

He lowered the paper he was holding. "I certainly would not choose to get involved with Napoleon were I a beautiful, married lady."

Patience fixed him with a glare. "You assume she had a choice. Perhaps the smart decision *was* to be involved with him."

Nate huffed. "Regardless of whether she is a smart woman or not, we can do little else but wait."

"In the meantime, she might be fleeing to London."

He shook his head. "We know she knows no one else. Where would she go? She is likely penniless and utterly alone. From those letters, it was clear she wished to see her cousin." He grinned as she began pacing again and thrust the paper at her. "Here, read this. You cannot pace and read at the same time."

"I'm in no mood for reading," she snapped.

He shrugged and tucked himself back behind his paper.

With a huff, Patience stomped out of the room. Let him sit and read, and be dull. She was not willing to do the same. After two days of sitting around and waiting, she was ready to tear down the walls. Especially when it meant being confined in a house with Nathaniel Kingsley. There was something about that man that made her want to simultaneously swipe that smug smirk off his face and then sit there and stare into his eyes all day and try to understand what made him tick.

Which was ridiculous. In spite of their conversation on the first night, she knew there was nothing spectacularly deep about him. Yes, he spoke of his brother and his desire to carve his own path, but honestly the man was doing that anyway. And he was mostly carving it through all the eligible ladies in Cornwall.

No, there were no secrets to be revealed about Nate. He was what he seemed—an arrogant, flirtatious, shameless rogue. She would learn nothing more from being in his presence.

Patience strode through the house and down the steps to the kitchen where Joyce had disappeared later that day. The acrid scent of something burning made her wrinkle her nose. As she entered the kitchen, she winced. A layer of smoke hung high up in the ceiling and the stench grew worse.

Joyce spun upon hearing her footsteps. Strands of dark hair stuck out at all angles from underneath a white cap and sweat beaded her brow. There were streaks of orange and black on her apron and a few smudges of black on her face. The evidence of this disaster was scattered across the kitchen in the form of copper pans on the stove, some revealing singed remains of what was perhaps once food, while flour was dusted across the table.

"You caught me," Joyce said, swiping her hands on her apron.

Patience scooped up some of the pots and placed them into the sink before grabbing a cloth, wetting it and wringing it out. She began wiping down the table.

"I can't cook," Patience said, "but I can clean."

Joyce grabbed a cloth to help with the table. "It's seems to be one of those days. Everything has gone wrong."

"Mistakes happen," Patience said softly, noting the real distress in Joyce's face.

"I cannot recall ever burning anything before. I do not know what's wrong with me."

Patience rinsed out the cloth and gave the table another wipe until all the debris was gone and the surface gleamed. She started work on one of the pots and grimaced at the charred remnants of food that was now glued to the bottom of it.

"If you show me, I can help if you would like. I could do with something to keep me occupied."

Joyce smiled. "Some help would be wonderful. I'm the same, I cannot stay still for long."

"Unlike Nate. He seems to have no problem sitting around."

"Lord Nathaniel does not strike me as a man who lazes around."

"He is doing a fine job of it up there." Patience thrust a finger toward the ceiling.

"You do not think much of him do you."

Patience frowned. That made her sound so condescending. Really Nate had done little to offend her if one ignored the rather lewd comments. His main fault was having agreed to help her brother and as much as she wanted to do this alone, she could not blame a man for wishing to help a friend.

"I do not know him that well," Patience explained. "We have lived in the same village all our lives but we've never had occasion to get to know one another."

"Well, now is your chance."

Patience blew a strand of hair from her face and scrubbed furiously at the pot. Flakes of burned food coated her hands in a satisfying way as she defeated the grime. Get to know him? She wished Joyce had not popped that idea back into her head. Had she not already dismissed trying to understand the depths of Nathaniel Kingsley?

"Do you think we are doing the right thing? Sitting and waiting for Pauline?" she asked after Joyce had finished putting away the clean utensils.

Joyce laughed. "I'm not the person to ask."

"You likely have more experience than I do in these matters if you keep house for government officials and suchlike."

"I try to stay out of the way. I'm happier cooking than I am getting involved in governmental affairs. As long as I can keep everyone well-fed, I am happy."

Patience envied the woman in many ways. To be so content with one's lot in life would be pleasant indeed.

"I cannot stay sitting around for much longer," Patience declared as she dried a pot and put it away. "We should be out finding her!"

"They are not your orders."

"Our orders are to get the information she has. No one said we had to pose as these cousins, merely that it was the simplest way. Well, frankly, I think it's daft."

Joyce tilted her head. "What do you intend to do?"

"A beautiful French woman will surely draw attention. Someone will know something of her."

"If you ask questions, you could draw unwarranted attention her way."

"I can be subtle," Patience insisted.

Joyce lifted a shoulder. "It is not my place to tell you what to do, my dear."

Patience grinned. "You will not stop me?"

"Stop you from what?" Joyce batted her lashes at her.

Resisting the desire to give the woman a big peck on the cheek, Patience rinsed off her filthy hands. "I shall help with dinner but once it gets dark, I intend to go out. You can tell Nate I am in my room with a headache."

"You will not be taking him with you?"

"I don't need a man getting in my way."

Joyce shook her head and smiled. "They do have their uses, you know."

"Not that man," Patience declared. "He is entirely useless."

Chapter Nine

Dinner had been a less ambitious affair of stew followed by custard in the end. It was hardly French cuisine but at least Patience's stomach was not rumbling and, if she was honest, after seeing the disaster in the kitchen, she had little appetite for something cooked.

She paused once she had slipped past the house and around the corner to tuck her hair into a floppy, slightly worn cap. It had belonged to her brother years ago, but given her size, it still fit her. The bindings around her breasts made breathing difficult but it was necessary. As Nate had so rudely and inappropriately pointed out, she was rather well endowed. If she was to remain inconspicuous, it was far easier to be an urchin boy than a woman in breeches. Thankfully the jacket she wore covered what the bindings could not quite disguise. She chuckled to herself. There was only so far one could crush one's breasts.

She made her way down the street toward the first inn she could find. Though she had visited Falmouth before, she could not claim to know her way around, so she forced herself to remember every turn she took so she could find her way back to the house with ease.

A chill wrapped about her, eating under the thin, battered jacket. A lamplighter worked ahead, climbing his ladder and lighting the way for her. There were still people on the streets but most of the well-to-do were at home, safely tucked in warm homes. A few bundles of fabric huddled into corners turned out to be homeless people with nowhere else to go. Patience shuddered, grateful she had a house to return to.

The amber glow seeping from clouded windows invited her in. The pub was crowded, mostly with men. A few women of loose morals clung to the necks of relatively well-dressed gentleman. A hoppy aroma imbued the air.

No one paid her any attention. She sucked in a breath and inched her way past some men playing an intense game of cards. Scattered goods were being gambled away including pocket watches, a ring, and even a set of teeth. Patience wrinkled her nose and made her way to the busiest part of the room.

Pressed up against the wall, she observed the scene before her. She had been to many travelling inns but never a pub like this. Now that she had the chance to stop and think about it, she was not quite that sure how she was to find out about this woman. None of the men looked at all approachable and most were deep into their cups. Perhaps if she simply waited and listened, she might find something out, though the din of laughter and masculine gossip that echoed through the building made it quite hard to distinguish anything of importance.

She waited until her feet and back began to ache, and a few people glanced her way before moving on. Patience continued this routine—visiting an inn, waiting around, hoping to spy someone who might look French or hoping for some tidbit of information. At the fourth pub, her efforts finally paid off. A lady of the night complained about someone with a French accent but the words were muffled by a loud bellow of laughter.

Swinging a glance at the women, Patience debated how to approach them and find out more. She need not have worried. A dark-haired woman approached, her dress low on her breasts and large amounts of makeup on. Patience stiffened.

"You look lonely," the woman said, her voice a low, husky tone.

"I-I'm fine, thank you."

"You have no drink or company. I've seen you looking my way."

Patience shook her head at the woman. Her dress was a deep purple and frayed around the arms. A simple comb held her hair back while curls spiraled haphazardly around her face. There was no doubting what she was, even if she had not spoken to Patience.

"I'm Rose," she said. "If you're looking for your first experience, I can give it to you. Many of the men here will tell you I am the best." She grinned. "And I'm cheap."

She shook her head again. "No, I don't need...that is...I am not here for my first experience." She paused and took a breath. "I was actually looking for a French woman."

Rose scowled and pursed her lips. "Why the devil would you want a French woman? Are English women not good enough for you? Aren't you a patriot?"

Patience had to bite back a laugh. If bedding English whores was the only thing that made one a patriot, she knew many people who were not.

"I have coin," she offered, "if you can tell me of any French women."

The woman's scowl softened. "You really fancy yourself a French bit of quim, eh?"

Certain she was pale as a ghost at the unsavory language, Patience dug out three shillings from her jacket pocket and handed it to her. "What do you know?"

Rose stuffed the coins into her cleavage. Patience tried not to think about how many other coins she might have there and how on earth she kept them safe. Surely when she undressed, coins would scatter everywhere? These were life problems that she had never had to consider before, for certain.

"Well, there are no French women here to be sure."

"That's all you know?"

The woman smiled and leaned in. "You shall cost me business tonight, boy. If it looks like I can't even sway a virgin lad into bed, what does that say about me?"

"How about we step outside and you can wait sometime before returning? Then everyone shall think I took up your offer."

She tapped a gloved finger to her lips, then nodded. Taking Patience's hand, she led her out through the front door and onto the street. The sides of the building were shadowed so they stopped there.

"How old are you?" Rose asked.

"It doesn't matter."

"Your hands are small," she said. "You're a bit young for a Frenchie I think. You really would be better off with an English woman."

"Rose, can you tell me about any French women locally?"

"I heard there was one by the docks. I don't know if she was actually a whore but it was said she bagged herself a rich fella." She huffed. "How come a French woman can get herself a rich man just like that?" She clicked her fingers. "I'm beautiful, and not daft in the head unlike some women. How come you all want bloody French women? There should be some kind of law that says they can't come here."

Patience hardly knew what to say. If this was indeed their French woman, they had a lead. She almost wanted to kiss the woman but certainly did not want to give her the wrong idea.

Rose eyed her. "Sure you don't want a quick fumble? You've paid me over what I charge anyway."

Patience shook her head vigorously.

"I'd be gentle, you know? If you think I'd be rough, you're wrong. Be sure to tell your friends that." The woman pressed herself up against Patience and leaned in. "I can be very, very gentle," she murmured.

Panic flared inside her. She glanced around for an exit as this woman—who was at least half a foot taller than her, loomed over her, lips pursed.

Abruptly the woman whirled away. Patience let out a breath but her relief did not last long. In the place of Rose was a bear of a man, his meaty fists curled. Hair sprouted from underneath his shirt and covered the backs of his palms. Patience could practically hear his heavy breaths as he pushed Rose behind him.

"Trying to get a cheap tup, eh?"

Patience shook her head.

"All deals with Rose go through me," the man said through gritted teeth.

As he stepped closer, the scent of his breath made Patience wince. Stale alcohol and chewing tobacco practically singed her eyes. A wiry dark bead covered his jaw and he sported a full head of hair, wild and untamed. Everything about this man screamed villain and somehow Patience had annoyed him.

"Sir," she held up her hands, "I had little intention of—"

"Liar," the man roared.

A crowd of people had begun to gather outside, eager to see what this mountainous man could do to this young lad. Crush her in half, no doubt. That would probably please Nate. At least then he could claim to be right, that they should have simply stayed and waited for the French woman to come to them.

Damn the man, she would not let him be right.

Patience lifted her fists, aware how small and ridiculous they looked next to the bearded man's.

"I wasn't going to tup her," Patience said. The word *tup* came out so meek and mild that the crowd laughed.

"You want a fight, lad?" the man sneered. "Do you have any idea who I am?"

"Um. No." She tried not to tremble as she peered around and looked for a way out. If she could just barge past him, she could run. Perhaps. If the crowd let her.

Or she could stay and fight and be ground to a bloody pulp. Either choice did not look particularly survivable. The man made the choice for her. He jolted forward and swung a fist. Patience darted back and felt the whoosh of air as his fist skimmed past her face. The crowd around them laughed. The man's face reddened even under the lamplight. A growl escaped him, just audible to her over the heavy thud of her heart.

"Sir—" she tried again.

He lunged once more, this time aiming his fist for her gut. She dodged to one side. Another punch and she ducked it. Further enraged sounds escaped the man.

"Keep bloody still!" he ranted.

Patience licked her lips. There was only so long she could dodge him. He was slow but all it would take was one direct hit to render her senseless. There had to be a better way to end it.

"Leave the boy be," someone declared.

Patience scowled. She recognized that voice. As she searched for it in the crowd, the bearded man brought a fist sideways to her face. At the last minute, she moved but it caught her hard enough so that her teeth rattled and her ears rang. She staggered back, clutching her jaw, and feeling as though it had to be ten times bigger than it should be. The bitter tang of blood swirled about her mouth.

The voice from the crowd stepped forward. Although dressed in clothes that were as shabby as her own boy's ones, it was not hard for her to recognize Nate. She stared, wide-eyed, as he stepped up to the man.

"What do you want?" her attacker sneered.

"Do you not wish to fight a real man?"

There was no disguising Nate's refined accent. No doubt the man thought Nate an easy mark. After all, in spite of Nate's muscular build—which she now knew far too well thanks to catching him shirtless in the kitchen—Nate was half the size of him.

The man smirked and nodded. "You're a lucky lad. Looks like he'll take the beating for you."

Fists raised, both men circled a little. Cradling her face, Patience watched in horror. What did Nate know of fighting except perhaps what he had learned in a boxing ring? But that was a clean fight. He would have never fought a man on the streets.

She needn't have worried. When the man leaped forward, Nate moved to one side and took hold of his arm. He twisted it backward, holding the wrist so that it was angled to the point that one slight move and it would snap. The man stiffened and let out a yowl of pain.

"Do you think perhaps you should leave the boy alone?" Nate gave his wrist another tweak.

The man yelped again. "Damn it."

"Well?"

"Yes, damn it, yes. Just let me go."

Nate released him slowly and swung a glance at Patience.

"Nate!" She saw his mistake instantly. He should never have looked at her. The bear of a man leaped on Nate and held him by both arms, pinning his hands behind his back.

The man nodded to several men in the crowd. "Who feels like warming up their fists tonight?"

No! Oh no, this could not happen. She had to do something. One man came forward and rolled up his sleeves. Nate wriggled against the man's hold but to no avail.

"Wait!" Patience screamed, the sound hoarse and piercing. "You cannot hurt him because..." She scanned the area for some way out but there was nothing. "Because I am a woman!" With a flourish, she whipped up her shirt, pulled down the bindings and watched as every man and woman's mouth dropped open.

The man's shock gave Nate enough time to escape. Patience dropped her shirt and dashed to him. He snatched her hand and pushed his way through the crowd. They dashed away until the crowd was far behind.

Heart still throbbing hard against her rib cage and a sharp ache in her jaw, she followed Nate. They kept a brisk pace, Patience near jogging along on his heels like a faithful pup, until they were far from the inn and nearly back to the house. He never uttered a word.

Nate stopped abruptly.

She stilled. "I know—"

He held up a hand and eased the other one under her jaw, lifting her face to the light. "You're going to have a mighty bruise. It's coming up already."

She nodded.

"Did you lose any teeth?"

She shook her head. Somehow, under his touch, the pain was already vanishing. She stared into a gaze that was growing intense. Her heart pounded harder than it had done during the fight, however that was possible.

"You have a little blood." He dabbed his thumb at the corner of her lip.

"A cut inside my lip I think. Nothing serious." Her voice came out horribly breathy. She hoped he didn't think it was because she was still scared.

And she had been, but she could never admit to that. Her brothers never felt fear, did they? Not when they rode into battle or spied on the enemy. She should not feel it either.

Nate gave a small sigh. "You are shaking."

"A little cold." Damn, she did not want him seeing her fear.

"You are likely a little shocked." He shucked off his scruffy jacket and slung it over her shoulders.

He began walking again and Patience hurried to catch up. "Thank you," she said breathily. "Thank you for your help."

"You were lucky I turned up on time."

"Yes," she admitted.

"You move quickly."

A tiny bubble of pride swelled and almost absorbed the frustration and humiliation that she needed a man to come to her rescue.

"I have always been fast."

"Do not do that again, though," he ordered.

She shook her head. "I won't." Once they reached the top of the steps to the house, she paused. "Nate, where did you get those clothes?"

"You're not the only one who can play dress-up, little one."

She wanted to ask more. *Where did you learn to fight like that? How did you find me?* But Joyce opened the door, looking a little sheepish, and Patience understood how he had tracked her down.

"I am sorry," Joyce whispered to her as she entered the hallway. "He's horribly persuasive."

Patience sighed. "Don't I know it."

Chapter Ten

Nate tried not to smile at the memory of Patience ducking and diving that brute as she sat opposite him in the breakfast room. In fact, the sight of a large, purpling bruise on her face should have made him furious. If it were any other woman, perhaps he would be, but not so with Patience. And that was not because he did not care she had been hurt, but more because he had seen what a scrappy little thing she was. Had he not turned up, she might well have come out of it just fine. He had never met a woman like her.

Breakfast consisted of a veritable feast compared to the dinner the previous evening with meats, eggs and fish to be enjoyed. Joyce had confessed she had suffered a disaster in the kitchen yesterday and Patience had helped—along with telling him where the damned woman was. It seemed the housekeeper was trying to make up for the lackluster meal. Nate slathered butter on toast while Patience covered hers in a generous helping of blackberry jam.

"How is your jaw?" he asked between bites.

"Tender," she admitted. "No more so than my pride."

He chuckled. "Your pride does not need to be tender. You're quite the fighter."

She giggled. "I'm not sure there was much fighting involved."

"Very well, you are excellent at evading punches. But any pugilist will tell you that's half the battle won, knowing when to dodge a punch. Were it not for you, I would probably be sporting a fine bruise too."

A rose redness sprung up on her cheeks. She leaned in, glancing around as though people could be listening in. "I hope we can forget last night."

"Of course," he said, adopting his most gentleman-like pose.

She nodded with satisfaction.

Good, she believed him. Because there was no way in hell he'd forget the sight of her baring her breasts, even if he'd only caught the briefest of glimpses. It was enough to remain embedded in his brain for life. Patience was steadily turning him into a breast man—or more specifically a Patience's breasts man.

He poured a cup of coffee and left it black. He needed the bitterness to keep him awake. After a night obsessing over Patience and her assets, his head was gritty. "Where is Joyce this morning?"

"She made breakfast then left to send a message to her sister."

"I've been thinking..."

"As have I."

"You were right to ask around."

"I know." She gave him a far too smug smile. "The woman I was speaking with—the one that nearly had me beaten to a pulp—said there was a French woman down at the docks and that she had been seen with a wealthy man. I think it's her."

Nate digested this information. It was hard for any French person to go unnoticed in England, not with the war. Most would be suspected of spying or worse.

"Think about it, Nate. She's a clever woman, used to using men to get ahead in life."

"You've met her, have you?"

She gave him a stern look. "I only know what I would do if I was in her position."

He lifted his brows. "Oh really?"

"Not that I would ever become an emperor's mistress or that any man would want me as one, but you know what I mean," she blustered.

Though tempted to try to flatter her, he didn't think she would want flattering. In fact, he was not at all sure what Patience wanted apart from to prove herself to her all-male family. It was odd indeed not to understand how to charm this woman. When had he ever struggled to enchant a woman?

Never. Not once. Not even when he'd been a young, scrawny man with a breaking voice.

"So you believe our Pauline has taken off with a man. Why go from Napoleon to her bastard husband to another man?"

"She needs shelter, protection, time, and she would not settle for living in the slums. This is an emperor's mistress, Nate. She is used to being spoiled."

"How do we track this man?"

"I suggest we go to the docks. Speak with some of the workers. Perhaps we can even discover which ship she came in on."

He took a long gulp of coffee. "I cannot fault your logic."

Her smile grew more smug.

Nate shook a finger at her. "Do not go running off on me this time. We both know how well that ends."

She gave a huff. "I won't go alone, I promise."

"You are a handful, Miss Patience Grey."

"And you are hardly the first person to say that."

"Am I the first to say that I rather like that in a person?"

"That they're a handful?" The color that had receded sprung back into her cheeks.

"Yes. Of course, one has to have big enough hands..." Nate shook his head as he considered quite where he wanted to put his hands. "Never mind."

She narrowed her gaze at him. "You said we would forget about last night."

"Absolutely. Of course. Entirely forgotten."

Her gaze narrowed in on him and he threw up his hands. "Utterly forgotten. No one shall ever know. It shall be our secret."

"How can it be forgotten if it's our secret?" she demanded.

"Well, almost forgotten then. Buried deep down. Come on now, Patience, do you really expect me to entirely forget that you saved my skin by way of flashing a little of your own?"

"Yes, if you were a true gentleman, you would."

"Patience, no true man could ever forget that, even the most gentlemanly of them all. If he did, I would suggest he was dead or insane."

"For goodness sakes, you act as though you have never seen..." she dropped her voice, "breasts before."

"I have never seen yours before," he pointed out. "At least I had not. I have to say, they lived up to all my expectations and more."

She sucked in a sharp breath and stood. "You really are the worst of men."

Nate lifted a shoulder. "If that is true, then why are you so flattered?"

"Flattered?" she spluttered. "Flattered by you making such lewd comments? I might not look much like a lady but I certainly never expected such comments."

"Never expected, but certainly enjoyed."

She threw down her napkin. "You are despicable."

As she stormed out of the room, Nate let a smile slip across his face. He might not understand how to charm Patience but he understood one thing, she was not immune to flattery. Buried under those masculine clothes and that stompy little walk was a woman—one who wanted to be called beautiful and appreciated for her sexuality.

Now all he had to figure out was why exactly he wanted to be the one to call her beautiful and maybe even appreciate that sexuality.

"If you wore a dress, we would not get so many looks."

Patience swung a sideways glance at Nate and ignored him. A fresh breeze twisted through her hair, ripe with sea salt. They took a turn through a tight alleyway that brought them out between an inn and a shoemakers. The buildings leaned in close together and cobbles, worn from years of use, slipped between them. Above, several lanterns hung from the eaves of the bottom story, presumably to light what would be a dark alleyway at night.

When they emerged, they were confronted by the road that ran along the dock to bring goods in and out. Although it was not a far cry from their own town, this was a bigger operation. Most of the supplies for Cornwall's towns came in through Falmouth. The docks were deep enough for ships bigger than even Nate's brother's and occasionally soldiers shipped out to France from here when they wanted to be assured of a quick, safe journey without fear of running into any French fleets.

There were no war ships in dock today, though. Several merchant ships were about, their masts rising above the smaller fishing boats. Wagons drawn by horses and donkeys crossed the road that ran all the way along the dock to the end of the town where they could then make their way to the other towns or to be loaded onto other vehicles or stowed in buildings.

Patience looked left and right as they covered the distance between the dock edge and the buildings. Amongst what were likely storage buildings were more shops and she counted at least another three inns, no doubt popular with the men coming off the ships. About them people moved with brisk certainty. It had seemed an excellent idea to come down here and find out more but now she saw the hustle and bustle of it all, she was not even sure where to start.

Nate paused and took a moment to peer up the dock. "That way," he said, pointing to the right. She spotted a big merchant ship, its sails raised, looking as though it was ready to depart at any moment.

"Why?" she asked, scurrying to keep up with him.

"I know that ship," he said.

"He works with your brother?"

He grinned. "Something like that."

They made their way along the dock, avoiding the unloading and loading of goods going on about them.

"Watch out, lad," someone shouted at her as she nearly knocked a box out of his hands trying to keep pace with Nate. "Uh, miss," he mumbled after looking at her.

"See, you should have worn a dress. People would not trip over you then."

"When you are as small as I—" she sucked in a breath. Why did the man have to walk so damnably fast? "When you are as small as I, people trip over you regardless of what you wear."

"I doubt they would trip over a well-dressed lady."

"I do not suit dresses, I'm not comfortable in dresses, and I would rather be tripped over one hundred times than wear one."

"So you have never worn a dress?"

"Of course I have. I could hardly attend balls in breeches or pantaloons now, could I? Why, we have even attended balls together where I have worn dresses. But, of course, I would not expect you to notice."

"No, why would I notice such a short person?"

She let out a huff, aware he was trying to rile her. He was succeeding, damn him. Why did he love to tease her so much?

"Nate." she called as she fell behind. "Nate!"

He paused and twisted on his heel, waiting until she caught up.

"Must you walk so fast." She drew in a breath. "As you have noticed I do not exactly have the longest legs."

And he seemed to have the longest ever. He strode with utter grace and confidence while she bumbled along, looking like a child trying to catch up to her father. God, she wished she was taller.

Once she had asked her brothers to try to stretch her. Jacob had grabbed her arms while Edward had grabbed her legs. They had pulled with all their might until she was in tears and they declared there was nothing they could do—she would always be as short and as stubby as a mushroom.

Nate glanced down. "It's hard to tell in breeches."

She gave him a look. "If you tell me you would be able to tell better in a dress, I would call you a liar."

"Not at all. I'm simply saying that the breeches are distracting. The way they...cling to you. It's hard to focus on the actual length of your legs."

"Are you truly trying to be rude again?"

The gall of the man! Was he making yet more comments on her figure? And why? No one had even acknowledged she had a body let alone made some sort of lewd comment about it. The only time people spoke of her was to complain that she was in men's clothing again.

He shrugged. "What can I say? I cannot help myself."

"Well, try," she snapped.

"I'll be on my best behavior from now on, I promise."

"Somehow I suspect your idea of best behavior and mine are a little different."

"Perhaps," he admitted, his grin far too rakish and appealing for her liking.

"Never mind, I shall take what I can get."

They stopped outside the merchant ship. The black painted hull gleamed in the early morning light. The autumn sun was low on the horizon and would remain so for most of the day if the skies remained clear. Nate stopped one of the men who was loading the ship with supplies. The man peered at him with suspicion then looked at Patience. He took in her appearance and his scowl deepened.

"Is the captain aboard?"

"Yes," the man said, hesitantly.

"Will you request an audience with him? My name is Nate Kingsley. He knows me." Nate gave the man a look that Patience did not quite understand. "I know his business well."

A flicker of understanding lit in the man's eyes. "I'll speak with captain," he said, hastening up the gangplank with a box of supplies.

"What did you mean, you know his business?"

Nate gave an overly innocent look. "These merchant men are suspicious types. I was simply telling the fellow that I was not here to steal business or cause some mischief."

She scowled. "That wasn't at all what it seemed like," she muttered.

Nate ignored her comment and the man eventually reappeared and waved them on board. He led them down into the bowels of the ship. It smelled of grease and sweat. Patience had been around ships all her life yet had never actually had the occasion to step on one. It was as cramped as she'd expected.

The captain's cabin was a little more generous than the living quarters they had moved through. With enough space to fit a desk and several chairs as well as a bookcase with worn books and leaflets filling its shelves, the large lamps and small port holes lit it well enough.

The captain was a small man, though he still had several inches on her. With thin dark hair, a slender face and boney hands, there was not a single part of him that could be called anything other than scarecrow-like. He offered a hand to Nate.

"Lord Nathaniel, what are you doing in my neck of the woods?"

"A little bit of business and pleasure," he said vaguely. "May I introduce Miss Patience Grey. Her father was Colonel Archibald Grey. You may have heard of him."

The captain gave her a glance over and somehow managed to keep the surprise from his face when he noted her appearance. Not that she was unused to such looks. At home, that happened rarely but here, they had likely never seen a woman wearing men's clothes.

"I believe I have. Quite the man. Captain Phillip Taylor at your service."

"It's a pleasure to meet you, Captain. How is it you know Lord Nathaniel here?"

Nate gave her a sharp but not quite annoyed look. She resisted the desire to stick her tongue out at him.

"His brother and I have done business once or twice," the captain said smoothly.

Too smoothly for Patience's liking. Something about this whole thing was odd but she could not say what.

"What can I do for you, Nate?"

"We're looking for a woman—a French woman. She came into Falmouth potentially a few weeks ago. We've been trying to track her down but with no luck. A source told us she was seen in the area, maybe soliciting for company."

The captain nodded. "French women hardly go unnoticed around here."

Patience straightened. "So you've seen her?"

He shook his head. "Not seen, but several men were talking of a fine, accented woman. Though she would have nothing to do with them. They say she was seen on the arm of a well-dressed gentleman and never seen again. The chances are she found herself a rich sponsor for the time being."

"Do you know anything about the man?" Nate asked.

"Nothing specific but if he was spending time here, you have to assume he has a ship. The biggest ships to come in here are for the Harrison Shipping Company. If I were a woman in want of rich company, the owner would certainly be the sort of man I would target."

Nate grinned. "I bet that's our man."

Patience nodded. "I think so too. We had better find out who it is."

"*I* will find out who it is, *you* can return home."

Eyes narrow, she glared at him. "Why would I return home and wait for you when I could be asking questions with you? You really do think of me as the little wife, do you not? I should be sitting at home, waiting with baited breath for your return."

Nate and the captain shared a look but Patience couldn't bring herself to care. She was not going to be forced out of this investigation.

"No," Nate said slowly. "But if Lord Nathaniel Kingsley is going to make enquiries about the owner of a business he might be interested in investing in, it would look better if he was alone and not accompanied by an unmarried woman in breeches."

"Oh."

"Yes, oh."

Patience dropped her gaze to her boots and waited for Nate to stand before she followed suit. "Thank you for your help, captain," she said meekly.

They made their way off the ship and Patience reluctantly met Nate's gaze. "I suppose I shall see you at the house then."

"Yes, and, little one, do not go getting yourself into trouble again. I could do without having to get into any more fights and I am sure you wish to keep yourself covered this time."

"Will you forever bring that up? I was trying to save you."

"And what an admirable job you did. I shall always be...grateful." His lips quirked.

What he meant was he would always remember it. Warmth struck her face for what had to be the hundredth time that day. She should be embarrassed—she was—but at the same time there was something horribly appealing about him thinking of her in that manner.

What a fool she was. Nate probably thought of thousands of women a day. She was just one in a whole blur of images.

She tapped his arm. "Go find out about that gentleman. And stop thinking about you know what."

"I shall try!" He gave her a jaunty grin and tapped the brim of his hat.

Damn that man. Damn, damn, damn, damn him. What were the chances that he was thinking of her breasts at this very moment simply to rile her? And why did she hope, so very much, he was?

Chapter Eleven

Nate had not expected to have to wait for Patience. Of all the women to be standing around in the hallway for, he never thought it would be her. How hard was it to put on a dress?

After expressing interest in Sir Magnus Colebrook's business dealings, Nate had managed to procure himself and a friend an invitation to one of his regular dinners. Magnus it seemed was new money—having risen from the ranks by dealing in coffee—and would not turn down patronage from a lord. Albeit a lord with a courtesy title. The invitation to dinner had arrived only a day after Nate had paid a visit to Magnus' offices. All was going well indeed.

He tapped a foot and pulled out his pocket watch. Well, it had been going perfectly until he told Patience she had to wear a dress. What she would say when he intended to tell people she was his mistress he did not know. Perhaps she was taking forever to punish him.

There was a creak from upstairs. Then a door closing. He held his breath and waited for that first footstep on the stairs. He watched avidly.

A slippered foot appeared, leading up to a column of frothy pink. He scowled. Then he nearly laughed. He clamped his teeth together—hard. So hard that his jaw hurt. After the hassle it had taken to get Patience into a dress, he would not laugh. He. Would. Not. Laugh.

Well, there went all his ideas of a ravishing beauty being underneath those breeches.

As she descended the stairs, she shot daggers at him with her gaze. "Do not say a word."

"You look...striking," he managed without laughing. "Like a beautiful...bird."

Very well, that was not his most charming of compliments but it was better than saying she looked like a pink blancmange that had been dropped on the floor and scooped up into a pile. Unfortunately for Patience, this hideous dress did her no justice. It hid her strong legs, sat awkwardly on her waist and somehow even managed to be unflattering to her breasts. The paler pink frills added width to her and the hue did nothing for her complexion.

He somehow managed to rip his gaze from the monstrosity and turned his attention to her face. If he did not look at the gown, the sight was quite pleasing. Gone was the practical hairstyle of a braid or some tight twist. Joyce had helped her he suspected.

Curls dangled around her cheeks, brushing them like the fingers of a lover. A few graced her neck too making it look long and succulent—ripe for kissing. A few white blossoms had been scattered throughout and a large gold comb held it all in place. Now if he could just forget the dress, he would have no problem pretending she was his mistress. Hell, if she was back in her breeches, he certainly wouldn't.

"You see now why I do not wear dresses."

"To be fair, I see why you do not wear *that* dress. I would have to see other dresses first to come to a proper conclusion as to whether or not you should wear dresses."

She made a face and wriggled.

"What's the matter?"

"I hate wearing stays."

Inwardly he groaned. So had she been corsetless this whole time? No wonder he had been unable to keep his attention from her breasts.

She gave another wriggle, handed him her reticule and gave the stays in question a tug through her dress. Once satisfied, she took the reticule and straightened her pelisse.

"Shall we?"

"The carriage is waiting." He motioned to the door. "It has been waiting some time."

"Well, if you had to wear stays, perhaps you would be late too."

He opened the door and escorted her to the carriage. "Some men do."

Patience opened her mouth and closed it. "No!"

A footman opened the door and they climbed in. Nate sat opposite her but he was beginning to regret it when not even the dim light of the lamps could hide that sickly pink color. Whoever gave her that dress should be shot. No, whoever made it should.

"Indeed," he said with a grin. "Some men like to keep everything in place." He patted his stomach.

"I had no idea." She glanced at his waist. "Of course, you will never have a need for that."

He thought color flew into her face at the mention of his body but he could hardly tell as the pink from the dress was reflecting off her face. He rather liked the bashful expression, though.

"I keep myself active," he agreed. "I would rather do a little exercise than wear women's underwear to be sure."

"If I had the choice, I'd never wear stays again."

If he had the choice, she wouldn't either. The thought of those breasts all confined made him slightly angry. They were far too glorious for such treatment.

"So," he said, in an attempt to move his mind away from where it had been lingering too much lately, "Sir Magnus has made his fortune in coffee. He lives lavishly and is obvious with his money. From what I heard at the docks, he likes female company."

"So it's likely he would take in an attractive French woman."

"Certainly."

"Let us hope she is there."

He nodded. "For tonight, we are not Mr. and Mrs. Smith, nor are we married. I am back to being Lord Nathaniel Kingsley and you are my mistress."

She opened her mouth and he held up a hand.

"I could not garner an invite as plain old Mr. Smith and if there is anyone there I know, they would recognize me instantly. Besides which, if Pauline has discovered her cousins are not in town, she will know we cannot possibly be them."

"But why your mistress? Can I not be your cousin or some such?"

"Patience, I hardly thought you the prim and proper type. Is it so very appalling the thought of being my mistress?"

"No. I mean, yes. Yes, of course. I would never wish to be your mistress. What a thought." She huffed out a breath.

"Anyway, if there is anyone there I know, they will know you are not my cousin, and the chances are there could be people I know."

She folded her arms. "I do not see how you are suddenly in charge of this all. You're not even a government agent."

"Neither are you."

"My brother is. He's taught me everything I know."

"Including dressing as a boy and getting into a fight?"

"No, but he taught me how to not get hit."

"He did a fine job. He would be proud. But now is not the time for fighting. We must wine and dine and be charming so we can get close to Pauline if she is there."

"I am not a simpleton," she said with a defensive pout gracing her lips. "I can behave."

"We shall see."

"I can," she insisted.

Oh challenging her was far too much fun. He had never really paid much attention to her at the various balls and events in the village but he was certain while her family allowed her to behave a little differently, they had taught her at least a little etiquette. She would not show them up. That dress, however, was another matter... Damn, the desire to take her to a dress-maker was unbearable. If they trussed her up in beautiful silks, what would she look like then? Curiosity was going to eat into him all night and he was willing to bet he'd spent the night picturing her in all sorts of different gowns and costumes.

Sir Magnus' house was not far from the property they were currently occupying so they arrived promptly. Set near the edge of the busy town, the house took up a large plot and was surrounded by wrought iron gates. Carefully tended green lawns and flower beds that likely bloomed with color in the spring followed the square lines of the house. Long windows glowed brightly into the night, revealing the shadows of occupants inside.

"Here we go," he said as he hooked Patience's arm through his and led her up the path to the front door.

A butler answered and led them inside. The entrance hallway had an air of grandeur but it was overdone. Every surface gleamed from golden framed mirrors to marble floors to busts of various Greek gods. Compared to his ancestral home, it was a lot shinier, but then the Kingsley home was full of antiques and old furnishings, and most had not been shiny for a long time.

After their coats had been taken, Magnus entered the hallway to greet them. With long thick sideburns and a full head of sandy hair slightly touched with red, the years of hard work hardly showed on his face. Only the creases around his eyes and slight dark shadows indicated he spent many nights working late to achieve all he had. Nate knew well enough about late nights but of course the sort of work he did was not quite so honest as Magnus'.

"Lord Nathaniel," he greeted, "I am mightily glad you could come. Nay, honored," he corrected himself. "I am honored you could attend my little soiree. It is nothing big but I do hope you shall enjoy the food and company. We are hardly like the set in Town but we do our best, and my cook is one of the finest at this end of the country."

Nate blinked, waiting for the man to take a breath. When it seemed he had stopped, Nate smiled and introduced Patience as his very good friend. Magnus hardly seemed to notice the pink dress or in fact the woman—his full attention was on Nate.

"Will you not come in? We are having drinks before dinner is served."

Nate followed Magnus, keeping Patience securely on his arm. He sensed the tension inside her but whether that was because of the situation or those damned stays, he could not tell. He felt the need to keep her close in case she did something reckless.

In attendance were several local families. He recognized a few but he had never been good at remembering the names of all these people he was introduced to. Balls were a bore unless a conquest-to-be was in attendance and although he did his duty and danced with a few eligible women and talked with those he must, he always felt as though he was not quite occupying his body. There were so many more interesting things to do.

But at least tonight was not simply a dinner party. Tonight he was on a mission and that was enough to ensure he paid attention and noted everyone's names. As Nate glanced around the room, he noted one woman sitting by the fire alone. With dark hair, fine, fashionable clothes, and an attractive figure even when sitting, he was certain she was their woman.

"Oh," Patience said.

"Is something the matter?" Magnus asked.

"Oh no, not at all. It's just... I see you have a Rembrandt." She motioned to the painting on one wall. "He is one of my favorites."

Magnus's eyes sparked and he seemed to finally notice the woman attached to Nate's arm. "You like art?"

"Indeed, my mother is quite the talented artist and was determined to teach me all she knew. I unfortunately did not inherit her skill but I certainly inherited her love for the greats."

Nate tried not to stare, really he did not. Where had this woman come from? And all this talk of art, was this true?

"Do you have any other pieces?" she continued, unlinking her arm from Nate's. She mouthed something to him but he did not catch what it was.

"Yes, I am quite the collector," Magnus said, his face as eager as a puppy's about to get a pig's ear.

"Will you show me?"

Magnus glanced at Nate, as though looking for permission. Nate nodded though he was still not sure what was happening.

Patience gave him a smile. "Why do you not get a drink, my love, and enjoy the company?" she said company tightly and swung her glance over at the would-be French woman.

Nate nearly slapped a hand to his forehead. Patience wished for him to speak to the woman. If he spoke to her without Magnus, perhaps he would find out everything they needed to know. Why he was being so dim-witted he did not know but he was certain the blame fell at Patience's putrid pink shoes and how her act had utterly befuddled him.

The use of *my love* had baffled him a little too.

"Yes, of course. I am no art-lover I'm afraid," he confessed. "You must show Patience here what you have or I shall never hear the end of it."

"I would be delighted. It is not often I get to discuss art with an expert."

"I am hardly an expert, sir, but I shall try my best."

Patience near led the man off so Nate took a drink from the footman and did a casual stroll around the room, pausing to speak with a couple he had met once before at a summer ball apparently. When he had finished with pleasantries and engaged them in enough conversation, he moved around to the fire and placed his glass of brandy on the fireplace.

The woman watched, an eyebrow arched.

"We have not been introduced. It was remiss of Magnus."

She smiled. "I am not an official guest." Her accent gave her away immediately as French.

"Lord Nathaniel Kingsley at your service."

"Sabine," she said simply.

So either this was Pauline and she was using a different name or this was another French woman. He wasn't sure that was particularly likely.

"How do you know Sir Magnus?"

She folded her hands in her lap and eyed him through a clear but calculating gaze. He had the impression she was taking in everything about him and weighing it up in her mind yet she revealed little in her expression aside from a hint of a smile. Patience had been right—Pauline, if this was her, was a clever woman.

Hell, he'd never hear the end of it.

"I am his mistress."

It was hardly rare for a man to take a mistress. After all, Nate himself had just strolled in with a supposed mistress on his arm. If the woman was a widow or high-ranking, one could get away with almost any indiscretion. Many a noble man took his mistress everywhere. However, he had not expected her to come out with it so boldly.

"And you have known him long?"

Her smile expanded a little. "A mere week."

"Ah. Is that long enough to be considered a mistress?" He moved to sit on the chair next to her.

"What else would you call me then?"

He shrugged. "A close friend?"

She laughed. "I do not think close friends behave quite as lovers do."

"Perhaps you are right. You are French, are you not? How are you finding it in England? Do people treat you well?"

Pauline or Sabine stiffened. "People treat me well enough. There are of course those who would think me a spy or some silly nonsense."

"You are certainly far too beautiful to be a spy."

"A spy cannot be beautiful?"

"Not at all. No one could forget your face."

"Is that why you singled me out, my lord? Because you find me beautiful?"

"I thought I had been quite subtle about it but apparently I was wrong." She giggled. "I singled you out because I was curious as to why I had not been introduced to you and why you were sitting alone."

"I am sitting alone because I am a French mistress in a room full of English people and Magnus is forgetful. He is very keen to show off all he has and I am not included in that."

"Seems odd to take a beautiful mistress and not wish to show her off."

She lifted a shoulder. "Magnus is a strange man."

"Not too strange for you, though."

"Life is often strange, *non*? I am not afraid of oddities."

"It seems Magnus has lucked out indeed to find a mistress like yourself." Nate stood to retrieve his drink and motioned to the drinks table. "Can I get you something?"

"*Non, merci.*"

"How long have you been in England?"

"Long enough to make me miss France."

"Why did you come here then?"

Pauline appeared to debate answering then she paused. "I would like that drink after all."

Nate fetched her a wine and by the time he had returned to Pauline the dinner gong was rung. He led the party in, as per his rank, alongside a Lady Rosa, the wife of a baron. Patience and Pauline were taken into dinner near the back of the line. Nate found himself sitting frustratingly too far from either woman. Of course, he should have been more bothered by being unable to sit by Pauline but he wanted to tell Patience of his conclusions.

Even if it did mean sitting next to that pink monstrosity, he also found it hard not to be able to talk to her. Apparently he had grown used to being told off every two minutes by her. He noted she swung the occasional glance his way but he suspected it was merely because she was itching to find out what he had discovered.

Of course, he had nothing solid—not yet. And Pauline was being careful, but if she had nothing to hide, why would she have skirted his questions? Why would she take up with a man she hardly knew? It had to be her.

But what now? Confront her? Wait? She was so close to running away and hiding under her shell he had to conclude they could not confront her so the only other option was to gain her trust, which would be a much longer game than they were expecting.

Funnily enough, however, the idea of extending his time with Patience did not bother him at all. She met his gaze and gave him a small smile. Did she feel the same, though?

Chapter Twelve

The whole affair reminded Patience why she loathed dinner parties. All that pretense. She suppressed a shudder.

By the time dessert was served, her cheeks hurt from a false smile and her back ached from sitting 'properly'. She could never fathom why people inflicted dinner parties on themselves and others. Making polite talk with someone she had never met and likely had nothing in common with was a bore.

Both men on either side of her were pleasant enough and did their best to engage but there was little they could discuss other than weather, Cornwall and the war. The baron to the left of her did his best to make witty remarks but, unfortunately, he was not a great wit, even if he was a sweet sort of a man. The other man— whose name she could not recall—had a drier sense of humor. She suspected he could be funny if not constricted by the rules and regulations of the dinner party.

Regardless, Patience was not interested in either of them. Only two people at the table held her attention and one of them should not have had it at all. She skimmed her gaze between Pauline and Nate, with it landing far too often on the latter. He glanced up and caught her eye occasionally and the oddest twisting sensation would burst into her stomach.

What was worse was that she found she liked that sensation. That she liked meeting his gaze. That in his finery with his cravat perfectly tied and his jacket near molded to his body, she found herself growing overheated when his blue gaze connected with hers. There had never been any denying Nate was a handsome man but any thoughts of denying she was unaffected by it were gone. At some point during their acquaintance, she had become far too aware of Nathaniel Kingsley.

With dinner finished, the men escaped for brandies while the women gathered back in the drawing room. While Patience mourned not being able to see Nate or talk to him about his conversation with the maybe Pauline, she welcomed the opportunity to get the woman alone. Perhaps she would confide in another woman, perhaps this could all be over tonight and she could go home triumphant.

The thought buoyed her and she practically skipped to take a seat next to the French woman.

"We have not been properly introduced. I'm Patience."

"Sabine." The woman cast a steely gaze over her, one brow arched. "You are Nathaniel's mistress?"

"Um. Yes. That's me."

"I would have thought he would dress you better."

Patience drew in a breath. Thoroughly aware her dress was hardly the finest of fashion, she had been loath to wear it tonight. Of course she would rather be in pantaloons but there was little to be done about it. This pink dress was about the only evening dress she owned.

"He, um, has unusual taste," she said, twining her fingers together.

"Indeed he does." That dark intimidating gaze ran over her again making Patience all too aware that this glamourous woman with feathers in her hair and a dress so exquisite it almost made her rethink not wearing gowns was the sort of woman Nate would like.

And certainly not someone like her with stumpy legs and no waist and terrible taste in gowns.

Patience lifted her chin. This woman might be who they were after—might—but she would not be intimidated or insulted by her.

"Of course Nate appreciates other things about me. He is not a shallow man. He enjoys my wit and conversation." Patience gave a secretive smile. "And my other skills of course."

Sabine threw her head back and laughed. "Ha, of course. I knew there must be something special about you for you to have secured such a man as your lover. I do admire a clever woman who can use her skills to her advantage."

"Is that what you did with Sir Magnus?"

Sabine waved a hand. "Pfft, he was easy to sway, though I suspect he does not know what to do with me now."

"Do you not want a lover who pays you attention?"

She shook her head, sending feathers bobbing back and forth. "I do not need a man's attention, merely his protection."

"Protection from what?"

"Why, life as a woman of course."

Patience hardly knew how to respond to that. The words struck her deep. Life as a woman. How unfair it was that by virtue of your sex, your life was made harder. As much as she longed for so much for herself, at least she did not have to foist herself off on uncaring men. For that, she had to be grateful.

"Someone mentioned you had only recently come across from France."

There was a visible stiffening of the woman's spine. "Yes."

"Did you leave a lover there?"

Sabine smiled. "And a husband."

Patience feigned shock. The comment sealed it in her mind, however. This had to be Pauline. "Will he not come after you?"

"I hope not. When I get the chance I shall file for divorce but for the moment..."

"You are hiding?"

Pauline glanced around the room and lowered her cup of tea with a sigh. "He was not a good man. He found out about my lover and was angry. I could not remain."

"Or he might have harmed you?"

Pauline nodded.

Cautiously, Patience reached over and laid a hand over hers. She drew in a breath. "I know all about your husband, Pauline."

The woman's startled gaze snapped up to hers.

"And about Napoleon," she whispered. "I'm here to help you."

"Help me?" She stood so quickly that tea sloshed over the side of her cup. "Help me. *Mon dieu*, you cannot help me, no one can, and if you think I would trust an English woman, you are beyond mad."

Without warning, Pauline grabbed her skirts and raced to the door. Patience did the same but the doors to the other drawing room swung open at the wrong moment and a crowd of men entered her path.

She pushed her way through but Nate grabbed her arm. "What's happened?"

"Pauline," she said, motioning frantically to the door where the woman had vanished. She wrenched her arm from Nate's and hurried after her. Nate's footsteps followed behind but she didn't stop to wait. If they lost Pauline now, they might never find her again.

Patience barreled out onto the street and paused to look left and right. The road was busy with carriages and wagons as guests at the local inn and other houses headed home for the night. Ahead, Pauline hurried up the street. Cursing her dress as it seemed to twine around her legs like pond weeds, she bundled it in one hand and gave chase.

Pauline crossed the road before a carriage raced past. Several more carriages crowded the road and Patience took a breath. She had almost lost sight of Pauline. They couldn't lose her!

Someone shouted Patience's name. She rushed forward, intending to make the gap between the next two carriages but something hauled her back. A strong band of what felt like steel wrapped about her waist and dragged her away. Nate's arm held her firm and they tumbled back onto the pavement. She tried to wriggle away but he was having none of it.

"Patience," he said.

"Let me go, we're losing her."

"She's lost." Her elbow struck him in the gut as she tried to get away. "Damn it, Patience. She's gone."

"No." She fought again but he was too strong and large. When she began trying to pry his arm away from her, he rolled her over so that her back was against the hard ground. He pinned her with his body and he wrapped his fingers about her wrists.

She could go nowhere. He had her imprisoned.

"Let me go," she protested.

"Not if you're going to attempt to get yourself killed again."

"I would have made it."

"Sweetheart, you would have been crushed."

She was being crushed now by his body. Hard on top of her, she was aware of every inch of him from his strong thighs, one pressing between hers to his granite like chest, crushing her breasts. She could hardly breathe. Rolling her head to one side, she peered up at the empty pavement. Only carriages came and went but there was no sign of Pauline.

"You don't understand," she said, hating the crack in her voice. "You don't understand." To her dismay, hot tears welled in her eyes.

"It is not worth your life." Nate stared down at her, his gaze running over her face and most likely taking note of her tears. She hated them and hated that he saw them. Tears were a sign of weakness and weakness was not acceptable in her family.

"You don't understand," she mumbled again.

He released a wrist and fumbled in his jacket before pulling out a handkerchief. Nate dabbed the corners of her eyes and her cheeks. His tender actions simply made her cry more. No one had ever wiped away her tears. If she had ever cried, she did so in her room where her brothers could not see and tease her.

Nate shook his head and eased himself to sitting, then he dragged her into his hold. There, on the cold stone pavement, he tucked her against his chest so tightly that she could hear the powerful thud of his heart. He held her there, one hand keeping her captive against him while the other brushed up and down her back. She cried for some time, ugly, ragged tears that left her chest aching and sore, and her eyes hot and swollen. His shirt grew damp under her cheek.

Once she was finally able to take a breath without sobbing, she straightened and he handed her his handkerchief. She wiped her eyes and gave an unladylike blow before offering it back.

He laughed and shook his head. "Keep it."

Patience bunched it up in her hand and held it tight. "I am sorry." Her voice was harsher than she'd expected. She felt as though she had been washed in scalding water and pulled through a wringer.

"You do not have to apologize."

"I do. I have been difficult and foolish. If I had not been so keen to finish this job quickly, I would not have scared her away. Perhaps if we had done it your way and waited it out, she would have come to us."

"Are you saying I might have been right?" He grinned.

"Never." She sniffed and smiled. "But I am sorry I did not listen. I know you are doing this as a favor to my brother. I'm sure there are other things you would rather be doing."

"Not at all. There's nothing I like more than a bit of subterfuge with a stubborn woman." He skimmed a thumb over her cheek where an errant tear was making its way down. "What do I not understand?"

She sucked in a breath and shook her head. A sense of relief ran through her, left her feeling exhausted but better. All that crying seemed to have done her some good. But was she ready to talk properly about her family?

Nate waited, his gaze patient and understanding. It was odd to equate this man with the arrogant and rude one she thought she knew yet it did not surprise her he had these qualities.

"You know I wanted to do this to prove something to my family," she stated.

He nodded.

"But it is more than that." She pulled at a curl by her neck, twining it around and around her finger. She could not meet his understanding gaze anymore so she eyed the mucky hem of her dress, all too aware of Nate's arms still around her. "My father never wanted a girl. He was disappointed to have one."

"You cannot know that," he protested.

"I can. I even heard him say as much once to my mother when I was young before he died. She asked him to let me be more involved with him and my brothers and he declared he wished I'd been a boy."

Nate hissed out a breath. "Christ."

"So you see why I must do this? I must prove he was wrong about me. That women are just as good as men."

"Sweeting, you are easily as good as your brothers, if not better. They have had the advantage of being born male while you have had to fight for everything. I am sure if your father saw you now, he would be proud of you. I certainly would be if you were my daughter."

She snorted. "What have I done to make anyone proud?"

"You've carved your own path. You do not care what anyone thinks. You're strong and brave, and clever."

She hardly knew what to say to these compliments. When had anyone said such words to her? And to be called strong and brave and clever? Most women would probably rather be called beautiful or elegant but not her. Those words meant more than he could know.

"You are a surprising man, Nathaniel Kingsley."

He tilted his head. "How so?"

"Underneath that arrogant exterior is quite the charming man."

"I thought I was always charming."

"Your idea of charming and mine is entirely different I fear."

"Well I am glad I have discovered a way of charming you. I thought it might never happen."

She peered up at him. Their bodies were still close, tangled together while he held her. The scent of subtle cologne cocooned around her and she felt her heartbeat trip. When she peered up at him, his face was mere inches from hers.

"You wanted to charm me?"

Yes. Please say yes.

"Yes."

A smile worked its way across her face of its own accord. How ridiculous it was that she should want to be on the receiving end of his attentions. She had a lot more things to worry about than whether a lord should wish to charm her—and even though he had admitted he did, it meant nothing. Nate was likely used to charming every woman in the country with ease. A man like himself would see her as a challenge. She should not take stock in it.

Nate eased his arms from around her and stood. He offered her a hand. Patience slipped her hand in his, brushing down her skirts as she came to standing.

She grimaced. "I think this dress is ruined."

"Good," he declared. "Let us burn the thing and forget it ever existed." The genuine disgust on his face as he stared at the gown in question made her laugh.

He shook his head and put her hand through his arm. "Let us see if we can explain this away to our guest."

Chapter Thirteen

"So what is your plan now?" Joyce asked.

Nate gave up trying to eat the thick porridge that was the texture of nearly hardened tar and just as edible. He shoved his spoon back into it and watched as it sat upright. Patience had taken to helping Joyce with meals and as much as he admired her perseverance, the results were not the easiest to digest.

"We wait," Patience declared.

He nearly choked on his toast. "Wait?"

"Yes."

"You"— he pointed at her —"wish to wait?"

"Yes." She frowned at him as though she could not understand his confusion.

Gone was the putrid pink dress and he hoped he would never set eyes on it again. In its place was the plain white shirt, slightly open at the collar and grey pantaloons. They did not hug her body quite as beautifully as breeches but they were a welcome relief from the eye-singeing gown.

Patience ignored his stare and turned her attention to Joyce. "Pauline has no other relatives, correct?"

Joyce nodded. "We know of no others and it seems these distant cousins are what's left of her family from her letters."

"Pauline is a woman used to a certain lifestyle. I do not believe she would simply run off and live off her wits."

"She might try to find another man to look after her," Nate pointed out.

"She might, but if I were her, I would rather connect with family, particularly after what happened last night. She would be fearful of being spotted again. It's easier to hide with family who know of her situation."

"So you think she shall go to her cousins?" Nate asked.

"But does she even know they're gone?"

Joyce shrugged. "Who can say?"

Patience nibbled on the end of her thumb. "If she has not come here yet, she must have concluded they are out of town and that the house is being let."

"So she will remain in Falmouth until they return."

Patience sent him a smile that had his heart beating oddly. "Precisely."

It was her hair that did it he concluded. She had left some of the curls in and it had a softer look. He wanted to tug on one of those curls like a naughty boy teasing a girl he liked. It brought out the plumpness of her lips and framed her face perfectly.

"Nate?" Patience stared at him expectantly.

He blinked and forced his attention away from her lips. "Yes?"

"What do you think then? Shall we do it?"

"Uh. Yes. Definitely."

Joyce clapped her hands together. "Excellent. I shall spread word that you are leaving and the Smiths will be returning shortly. Then we just have to make it look as though no one is here. Either she turns up while you are supposedly gone, or we make it look as though the Smiths have returned and she searches them out then."

Nate tried to digest this. "How will we make it look as though no one is living here?"

"We cannot come and go, we shall have to leave the fires and lights unlit. Just for a few days," Patience said. "If she has been watching us at all, she will think we've gone."

Nate lifted his coffee cup in a mock toast. "Sounds like we have a plan."

Pain burst through Nate's knee. "Goddamn this bloody plan." He glared at the offending table leg that had decided to get in the way of his knee. With only a little light from outside seeping into the drawing room, he could hardly make out the offending object.

"Language," Patience scolded.

"Where are you?" He squinted into the dark to make out a huddled shape tucked up on the sofa.

"Over here."

"Over here," he mimicked. "Like I know where 'over here' is."

"There's no need to be so grouchy."

He made his way cautiously over to her voice, hands out to prevent any more accidents. It wasn't the first. They had been in hiding for two days while Joyce had spread word that they were leaving and she was closing up the house until the Smiths returned. In the meantime, Nate's limbs and toes had managed to find every bit of furniture in the deuced house. By the end of this, he would be covered in bruises.

"Nate, careful."

Her warning came too late. His shin struck the edge of the sofa and he toppled.

It took him a moment to realize quite what he had fallen on. His face was surrounded by something soft. So soft. And generous. Two shapes that seemed to cup his head.

"Nate."

"Just a moment," he murmured to her breasts.

"Nate!" Patience tried to push him off.

He finally eased away and found a spot on the sofa to sit on. "My apologies," he muttered, not feeling at all sorry. That was the nicest thing to have happened to him in days.

"It doesn't matter."

"Your night vision must be better than mine."

"I have been sitting here for a while. My eyes have adjusted."

He eyed her until the shape of her grew more visible. Wrapped in a blanket, she had her legs tucked up on the seat.

"What were you doing?"

"Trying to stay warm mostly."

It was odd not to be able to see her expressions. He did not much like it. He had not realized how expressible her face was until he could no longer see it.

"You should go to bed. Joyce has I believe."

"Joyce is a sound sleeper. Have you heard her snoring?"

Nate laughed. "I have." Despite there being a floor between them, the woman managed to wrack the rafters with her snoring at times.

"She can get to sleep no matter what. I am too... I'm not sure... I just feel like I am waiting."

"Yes, I know what you mean. It's hard to rest when you know something might happen."

"I hope so. I hope all this sitting about freezing is worth it."

He reached out tentatively, hoping he didn't get a handful of breast, as much as he would like it. Luckily, he found her hand and indeed her fingertips were freezing. She was so small, it was no wonder.

Nate edged closer and put an arm around her. She made no protest and lifted the blanket so it covered them both, which was a clue to how cold she had to be. Patience burrowed close. His heart felt as though it had doubled in size. All these strange heart movements and flutters were getting tiring. Why Patience brought out the protective side of him, he did not know. The last woman to need protecting was her. She was the toughest woman he'd ever met.

"Do you think this will work?" she asked, her head resting in the crook of his arm.

For a moment, he could not reply. She fit so perfectly there. It was as though he understood precisely why she had never grown tall. It was all because she was intended to fit against him.

Shaking away the foolish thoughts, he cleared his throat. "It's worth a try. You were right about her being a clever woman. I think you could be right about this."

"I hope so. I would hate to go home and tell everyone I failed."

"I know your brothers, they would not think you had failed. Besides, Jacob was asking a lot from you. Even trained operatives get things wrong."

"He asked a lot of you too but you don't seem concerned about failing."

He shrugged. There was no need to mention that he had more experience in the area of espionage than she realized. Of course, most of it was more to do with sneaking goods into the country but he had met plenty of spies since he and his brother had started smuggling. The amount of men and information they had snuck in and out of the country was too many to count at this point.

"I don't doubt we will find her."

"I wish I could be as confident."

"You should be. Together we will find her, we will get that information and we'll return home triumphant and if that does not make your brothers proud, then they are simpletons."

Patience yawned, a long, loud yawn that she failed to smother. "Forgive me, I am not used to being up so late. I'm normally an early riser."

"I tend to stumble into bed whenever I feel like it. Though once my brother marries Hannah, I have a feeling things will change."

"Will it be strange living with a married couple?"

"It does make me consider renting a house nearby. Breton Hall is available I believe."

"Does Lord Redmere know you wish to move out?"

"Not yet. I shall tell him once the wedding plans are finalized. He has a lot to worry about at present."

"And he worries for you," she stated.

"Too much. He forgets I am no longer a young man with no mother or father to look after him. Perhaps if I set up house on my own, he will realize."

"It seems we both have things to prove to our brothers."

Nate laughed. "Brothers, eh? Who would have them?"

"I do love mine dearly but I wish they would see me for what I am, especially Harry."

"And how do they see you?"

"As a child, I should imagine."

"I cannot see how they could not see you as a woman. After all you are extremely—"

"Do not even say it," Patience warned.

"Mature," he finished. "I was going to say—"

Patience cut him off by slapping a hand over his mouth.

"I was not being rude," he protested, the words muffled.

"Shhh. Did you hear that?"

Her hand still clapped over his lips, he forced himself to listen. There was a squeak, then a clatter.

"Could it be her?" Patience whispered.

"Mmmf."

"Oh." She removed her hand from his mouth. "Sorry."

"It might well be. I think it's coming from the kitchen."

"Yes." She scooted forward and stood. "Quickly," she ordered. "We must catch her."

With as much speed as they could manage in near pitch dark, they made their way down to the kitchen. Nate would have preferred to go in front but Patience would not let him take the lead. She paused in the doorway to the kitchen. With no curtains, it was the lightest room in the house with the basement windows dropping enough pale, shimmering moonlight for them to be able to see the layout of the room.

Nate peered over Patience's head into the room but could see nothing. Patience turned to press a finger to his lip, as if he could not be trusted to stay quiet. He was sorely tempted to nibble on that fingertip to teach her a lesson. Had another clatter not sounded from near the pantry he might well have. A shadowed blur zipped past them and Patience near jumped into his arms. She gripped him so tightly that he could feel her heart pounding against his chest.

"A rat," he hissed. "A damned rat."

"Shit."

He smothered a laugh at her unladylike expression. But before he could tease her for it, the rear door to the kitchen squeaked. Unwilling to let Patience take the lead any longer, he urged her back behind him and edged toward the door. It eased open, letting in a blast of frigid air. A figure stepped in and Nate positioned himself flat against the wall. Patience followed suit. Once the person had come fully into the kitchen, Nate moved to lock the rear door. The intruder spun at the sound of his footsteps.

Pauline's features were clear to see in the nightlight. She sighed. "*Merde.*"

Chapter Fourteen

Patience took full enjoyment of the lit fire in the drawing room. The sweet warmth licked into her bones as she eyed their bounty.

Pauline Fourès had fared well considering she'd fled the safety of her protector's home not long ago. Ever elegant, her pale pink pelisse and gown were perfectly pressed. Whatever she had been doing since they saw her last, she had been well looked after.

"I remember you," she said, her accent making her words sound almost lyrical. "You were *la fille* in that awful pink dress."

Patience glanced at Nate who was clearly suppressing a laugh.

"Yes," Patience said through gritted teeth. "That was me."

"I did not realize you were hunting me down," Pauline said with a huff.

She sat on the sofa, slightly reclined as if she did not have a care in the world. Her dark hair was carefully braided around her head and held up with a silver comb. It was as though she was at a party instead of being held by two strangers. A pang of envy rolled through Patience. How could she be so calm, so self-assured?

Pauline peered at her nails. "I suppose you want something from me?"

Nate nodded and strode forward. He set himself on the chair opposite and leaned forward, elbows on knees. Even Patience's heart did a little flutter at the movement of his lithe body and the intense expression on his face. Goodness knows how Pauline felt being on the receiving end of such a look.

"We want to protect you," Nate told her.

The woman peered at Nate for some time before straightening a little in her seat. Whatever magic Nate was wielding, it was working. Patience should have always let him take the lead on Pauline—after all he was quite the expert on women, she thought bitterly.

Pauline waved a hand. "I had protection."

"Sir Magnus was already tiring off you."

She snorted. "*Oui*, the fool. He hardly knew what to do with a woman. I had strong suspicion he was...well...you know." She smiled.

Patience frowned. "Was what?"

Nate shook his head. "It does not matter."

Pauline gave her a sympathetic look. "Poor, sweet girl. You are an innocent thing are you not?"

"Hardly," Patience protested, feeling innocent indeed.

Next to this vivacious, beautiful woman, she felt like a short, stumpy, ugly pig. No, make that a boar. A hairy, stunted, grunting boar. Each word out of her mouth felt stupid and nonsensical and every movement was awkward and bumbling. And Patience had hardly said a word or moved an inch yet!

"Where are my cousins?" Pauline asked.

"Out of town," Patience said firmly.

"And they will be gone for long?"

Nate nodded. "As long as we want them to be."

Pauline adopted a pout. One that made her look more attractive rather than sulky. The sort of pout that made a man want to fix all her woes for her. Patience caught herself pressing her own lips together in imitation and quickly straightened her mouth.

"You English are devious."

"Yes we are," Nate agreed, a gleam in his eye.

That gleam—the sort of wicked one that always made her want to slap him as well as fling herself against him—had a similar effect on Pauline. She seemed to rise to attention that little bit more.

The atmosphere grew thick. Patience tried not to grind her teeth. A long look ran between the pair and it took all her willpower not to jump between them and do something foolish. Thankfully Joyce entered before Patience sprang into action.

"Tea, my dears," she declared. "Tea and sandwiches. No warm food yet but I am working on that." The housekeeper's face lit up at the idea of being able to cook a proper meal. "I am sure you are all looking forward to that."

"That we are, Mrs. Rowley, that we are," Nate agreed.

"Well, I shall leave you to it," Joyce said, leaving the tray on the coffee table and backing out of the room.

Pauline leaned forward, her gaze on them both and poured herself a cup of tea. "I prefer coffee. Tea is so English."

Regardless of her dislike of tea, she sipped away quite happily before helping herself to a sandwich. Patience's stomach grumbled loudly enough for everyone to hear and her cheeks near boiled with embarrassment.

Pauline smothered a giggle and motioned to the food. "I shall not eat it all. I have to watch my figure."

Patience had never watched her figure in her life, unless it was to grumble with it in dissatisfaction at being so shapeless and short. There was little point. What help was a womanly figure when bounding across fields after one's brothers or going on a hunt? Pauline, however, used her assets to full affect, and Patience could not help wonder if she should not have spent more time wearing corsets and eating carefully—though with her height she could likely starve to death and not change one bit.

Ignoring the offer of sandwiches, Patience met the woman's gaze head on. She would not be intimidated by her. Not by her elegant figure or by her beautiful clothes. Not by her braids nor her long arching neck. Not even by the way she appeared as though she owned the place. They had a mission to complete and nothing would stop her. Heck, she had faced down the most brutish of men in her attempt to find Pauline. She had nearly been crushed by a carriage. She had lived in the freezing cold for several days and survived it all. No, there was no need for her to be intimidated by this woman.

"We want the information you have on Napoleon, Pauline," Patience said bluntly. "You are being watched. You have been watched for some time. You will not be allowed to leave until you give us that information."

Pauline eyed her for several moments, her lips pursed. "I like you," she finally concluded. She motioned to Patience's pantaloons. "You look better in those."

Patience opened her mouth, unsure how to respond to the sudden reversal in attitude.

"Will you help us?" Nate pressed.

A flicker of amusement teased the corners of Pauline's mouth. "Perhaps. What is in it for me?"

"Protection."

The woman laughed. "That information *was* my protection. Am I to trust the *English* with my safety?" She said English as though the very word pained her to say.

Patience finally sucked up the courage to sit next to Pauline and forget how inelegant she felt next to her. "You are being watched. Your letters were being read long before you came to England. There will be no escape for you until you give over the information."

"So I am to betray my fellow countrymen?" Pauline asked dramatically.

Patience fixed her with a look. "You were betrayed by Napoleon, were you not? And your husband? They do not deserve your loyalty."

A flicker of pain echoed in the woman's dark eyes before it vanished. She drew in a breath and released it loudly enough for them all to hear. "They do not, that is true. But how can I be sure I will be safe when this information is in the hands of the British? Napoleon will surely want me dead after I have betrayed him."

"Napoleon has enough to deal with at present. He will not bother himself with you," Nate assured.

"And even if he did, we can ensure you are safe," Patience added. "There are many places in Britain you can go. You will no doubt be richly rewarded for your service to your new country."

Pauline flicked her gaze between them both then leaned back in the chair. "I do not know if what you say is true but I want the English to stop following me, to stop reading my letters. If you can promise me at least that much, I shall tell you all I know."

Nate nodded. "That we can promise with ease."

"Very well." Pauline eyed her fingernails for a moment. Only the pop and crackle of the fire sounded. "I do not know anything myself. It is all in documents. Letters and suchlike. I left them at Magnus' house for safekeeping."

Patience blinked. "You left them behind?"

"Well I left in a hurry, did I not?" She gave Patience a pointed look. "But I was planning to get them back. If you let me leave I shall have them back to you with ease."

"No." Nate stood. "You will stay here until we know we have everything we need."

"We can get the information ourselves," Patience agreed, "just tell us where it is."

Pauline sighed and offered another pout. "You do not trust me I see." A smile played on her lips. "Very well, it is in his library. There is a book—*Candide* by Voltaire—you know it?"

They both nodded.

"You will find the papers in that book."

Nate rubbed a hand across his chin. "All of them? It's a small book."

"You shall find all you need," replied Pauline, jutting her chin up.

"I suppose I had better contact Sir Magnus. Let us hope our little display on our last visit did not frighten him off." Nate shot Patience a look that reminded her of the fact that she had chased off Sir Magnus's mistress and caused quite a to do, particularly when she had returned to the party looking more than a little flustered with no explanation as to why she had done what she had.

"If you are planning on attending another dinner party, you cannot send her in that pink dress again." Pauline nodded toward Patience. "I have some fine gowns in storage. She can wear one of those. That pink dress should be burned." The woman gave a mock shudder. "It is an insult to fashion."

"Perhaps I have other dresses, nicer dresses," Patience protested.

Pauline ran her gaze up and down her and shook her head. "*Non*, you do not. You shall wear one of mine," she said firmly.

Patience looked to Nate for him to come to her defense but he merely shrugged, an amused smile upon his face. Apparently she was going to have to wear yet another dress and there was nothing that could be done about it.

Chapter Fifteen

"Patience."

Patience turned so see Pauline poking her head out of the bedroom door. Although the woman was not confined to her room as such, Nate had insisted on ensuring he knew where she was at all times, and refused to let her walk around the house unescorted.

"Do you need something?"

"*Oui.*" Pauline pushed open the door. "Come in here."

Frowning, Patience entered the bedroom. With the curtains drawn, the room made a gloomy prison. Pauline insisted on keeping them drawn while she was in hiding lest someone recognize her. Lamps were lit in several corners but could not combat the feeling of the room being utterly stifling. Particularly for a woman like Pauline. Patience had only been in her company for two days while they waited for their chance to go to Magnus' for another dinner party but she had the distinct impression Pauline was not the sort of woman who could be confined. She could not help pity her for her situation, forever having her life dictated by men.

Pauline sat on the bed and patted the mattress. Patience let her frown deepen.

"Come here, you silly English girl. Have you never confided with your girlfriends before?"

She shook her head. "I have none."

"Well, you have one now." She patted the bed insistently.

Unable to protest or quite fathom what Pauline meant by *you have one now*, Patience sat. Did that mean Pauline considered her a friend? Her first female friend was Napoleon's former mistress?

What a riot she would have telling people in their village that. Of course, no one would believe her.

"You are different, are you not?" Pauline asked.

"Do you need to ask me that?" she indicated to her breeches.

The French woman laughed. "*Oui*, you are right." She gave a dramatic sigh. "I am the same. I was never satisfied with mere marriage and duty. And I will not be satisfied with hiding away in Scotland or some other frightfully cold place while under the protection of the British. I shall die from boredom, I am sure of it."

"I am sure they shall find you somewhere pleasant to stay."

"I cannot abide the thought of being watched over forever. I am sure they will still spy on me. You must know that, Patience."

Patience grimaced. The chances were Pauline would not be allowed to comfortably settle without any interference. She knew too much. There would always be people watching her, at least until the war ended—if it ever did.

"I do not know why you are telling me this, Pauline. I have no power over what happens to you."

"You have some power. Especially over Nathaniel."

Patience laughed. "He never listens to me."

"You are wrong. I see him. He watches your mouth so carefully, as if each word that comes from your lips is a treasure. He listens."

Shaking her head, Patience smiled to herself. If only that were true. She would dearly enjoy holding Nate's esteem. How she had gone from resolving to loathe him forever to wanting his esteem, she did not know, but there it was. She wanted him to like her, to think what she had to say held some importance. How fickle of her.

"You must speak with him. Persuade him I must go."

"We need to get the information first, Pauline. You know why."

She gave a sad sigh. "Ah, *oui*, you do not trust me."

"We put quite a lot of effort into finding you." Patience nearly laughed at herself when she considered the fight she had landed herself in and the days spent tripping around a cold, dark house. "Even if Nate were not here, I would not release you."

"But after?" Pauline asked hopefully. "What about after?"

"It is safer for the government to look after you. What would you do on your own anyway?"

"I have my cousins. They will return when you are gone. They can help me. I shall travel perhaps. There are ships enough around here. A warm country would be nice."

Patience shook her head slowly. "I am not sure what I can do for you."

"Let me leave when you have your information. Leave the front door unlocked. I can slip away. After all, I will not be needed then."

"Pauline, I—"

"Or better yet, come with me." Pauline's eyes were bright with excitement. "Come with me and we shall have wonderful adventures. You are not made for marriage or a dull life, I know that."

"Oh no, I'm—"

"We shall be safer together and you are strong, are you not? *Oui*, you are, I can tell. Strong and determined. Between us, we could do anything. And I like you, and you like me. It would be perfect."

"I really do not think...that is, I have a family. They would miss me."

"Your brothers? Pffft." Pauline waved a hand. "I heard you talking of them. They are too busy being men to care about their sister." She grabbed Patience's hand. "Come with me. We could have such fun."

There was a deliberate cough outside the door and Pauline dropped Patience's hand abruptly. Pauline stood, feeling as though she had been caught conspiring with the enemy.

"Think about it," the woman whispered as Patience hastened out of the room.

Nate stood in the hallway, arms folded. Creases marred his forehead and his expression was dark. Patience jutted up her chin and stalked past him. He followed her down to the drawing room. He had heard enough, she knew that much, but why he was angry about it, she did not know. After all, it was hardly her fault Pauline was plotting.

She picked up a poker and gave the fire a jab. Sparks popped from the logs. Behind her, Nate remained. She did not need to look at him to know that same dark expression remained on his face.

"You are not considering it, are you?"

She rolled her eyes, gave the fire one more stab then placed the poker back in its holder before facing him. She mirrored his stance, crossing her arms and keeping her legs slightly apart. She had not, until he had challenged her. Was it so astonishing a thought that she might wish to travel and experience excitement and danger?

"And what if I am?"

"Patience, you cannot be serious. We are to hand her over to the government, not release her into the wild."

"I cannot blame her for wanting to be free, Nate."

"And you? Are you not free?"

"How can I be? I am a woman. If I do not marry, I shall become a spinster and a target for pity."

"What of your family?"

She shrugged. "My brothers shall not miss me."

"Your mother will."

"She is too busy with her painting. Anyway, it is not a prison sentence. I could return if I wanted to."

Nate took several bold strides to close the gap between them. "Patience, listen to yourself. You wish to gallivant off to who knows where when you have never been farther than London—if that—with a woman who could very well be targeted by the French and British."

"Sounds fun," she said, well-aware it would rile him more. But why should he be so bothered? He was not her keeper or her *real* husband.

"You are too innocent, little one. You have spent all your life in a sleepy little village where everyone accepts that you wear breeches and turns a blind eye. You will not find the same welcome anywhere else."

"You think me horribly naïve, do you not? Well, I do not see how you can know much of the world either. We grew up in the same small village if you recall and I do not think trips to London and Scotland count as seeing the wide world. The life of a nobleman is hardly one filled with danger and adventure, is it?"

"Patience, you have no idea how much danger and adventure I have been a part of."

She laughed. "If you mean slipping out of married women's windows, I do not think that counts."

"No," he hissed. "I mean sailing across enemy-laden seas. I mean evading excise men. I mean smuggling in spies."

Patience opened her mouth, then closed it again.

Nate straightened and pushed a hand through his hair. "Damn it."

"What do you mean, excise men? And smuggling spies?"

He huffed out a long breath and pushed his glasses back up his nose. "I know more about danger than you will ever know."

"Nate?"

He motioned to the chair and she sat, eyeing him as she lowered herself down. Moving to stand by the fire, he rested an elbow on the fireplace.

"I should not have said as much. What I have told you could put many people in danger, particularly my brother."

"Lord Redmere?"

"He is the only brother I have."

"Yes, of course. Forgive me."

He stared at the flames for a moment. "I trust you, Patience, so I do not think I need to tell you this information is not to be repeated."

"I swear it."

"When I found out my eyesight was not good enough for me to join the army, I threw myself into drinking and well...other unsavory behavior. My brother feared that without a purpose, I would turn into another one of those useless second sons."

"I do not think you could ever be one of those."

He gave her a look. "I am a different man to what I was then. Perhaps I am even changed again since." He ran a finger along the mantelpiece and stared at the fire once more. "My brother wanted a way for me to be involved in the war effort and find purpose. By chance he came across a British spy sheltering in Penshallow. My brother helped him and that led to his current operation—which is smuggling."

She drew in a breath. Smuggling? Surely not. Everyone knew that smuggling took place in Cornwall. There was talk of the Ship Inn being a center for it, but no one had ever proven anything and most did not care enough to pry. But to suggest that the Earl of Redmere was involved...?

"Yes," he confirmed, as though she had spoken the words aloud. "My brother oversees a smuggling operation going out of our little village. He uses it as a cover to bring in information and people as well as take them over to France. It also means we can bring in goods that we are not meant to have." He grinned. "I did sorely miss French wine until we managed to get our hands on some."

Patience gaped at him for what felt like many moments. It was so hard to fathom. Nate was not this lackadaisical lord as she had originally assumed—though admittedly she was far from seeing him that way now. And Lord Redmere, well, he was practically a pirate!

"So you see, little one, I know much about danger, and I do not recommend it to you."

"But you will continue to smuggle?"

"Of course. As long as the war continues, we have a role to play."

"Why do you expect me to be satisfied with doing nothing then? We both know I shall not be given any other missions. This was simply luck that I was allowed along on this one."

"Patience, promise me you will not go with her." He thrust a finger at her. "Promise me."

She shook her head. "I cannot." What Nate did not realize was that his story had not put her off the idea but had persuaded her to think on it more. After all, if a lord could become a smuggler, could a young woman not become an explorer?

Chapter Sixteen

Nate could not recall ever feeling this nervous. Perhaps it was Patience in that dress that was doing it. Maybe it was because Knight and Drake had still not arrived. It could have been because they had to have dinner with Sir Magnus and somehow find a way into his library. He glanced at Patience. No, mostly it was the dress. Every time he looked at her, his hands grew clammy.

He tried to peer at the painting on the wall—a hunting scene—but his gaze inevitably tracked back to Patience who was, it seemed, as nervous as he. They had been pacing in the hallway for near on ten minutes, waiting for his friends to arrive.

Pauline could not be trusted on her own and as much as the housekeeper was determined she would not escape under her watch, it was unfair to ask the diminutive woman to watch over her. So Nate had sent word to his brother to ask for some muscle in the form of Knight. The response had been swift, coming by direct messenger. Drake, it seemed, wanted in on the action. Nate suspected it was more to do with wanting to meet this elusive French woman. The damned man could sniff out an attractive woman from twenty miles off.

He hoped Drake did not do any sniffing around Patience.

Damn, that dress. Who knew a little bit of fabric and lace could have such an effect? Of course, it was not just that. It was the way her hair was curled, making his gaze follow said curls to her long neck then down, down, down to her bosom.

How any man was meant to stay sane around such a bosom, he did not know. They were hard enough to ignore in shirts but the squared neckline of the green silk gown was designed to tantalize. Every time Patience took a breath, he marveled at how her breasts did not spill entirely from the garment.

In she breathed. Any time now, he told himself. Any time now, her breasts would just pop out, and yet they did not. She exhaled and her breasts remained perfectly in place. Whether his sanity lingered was another question altogether.

Patience tweaked the lace of her sleeve, clearly uncomfortable in the dress. It was not, he concluded, the first time he had realized there was something innately attractive about Patience, but it was certainly the first time he had realized she was capable of being feminine. And, in truth, she would be rather good at it if she did not fidget so much. Yes, she was still small and did not have that long column like figure or waifish waist so many women hungered after but she was utterly, and innately appealing.

Since their conversation the other day, they had not talked about Pauline's offer. He secretly hoped Patience had forgotten the idea entirely and then any interference would be unnecessary. He could not allow Patience to run off with Pauline, he simply could not.

The knock at the door was a welcome distraction from Patience. If he remained in the hallway with her for much longer, he was not sure what he would do—something extremely irresponsible and roguish most likely.

Drake and Knight stood at the door, water dripping from the brims of their hats. A light rain had started up, making the steps leading down from the house gleam. He peered around them for any sign of another visitor but there was none. Nate did not know whether to be relieved or not. Patience would not be happy when she found out what he had done.

"You could have warned me about the steps," Drake said, his grin belying his grumbling tone.

He tapped his leg that on bad days was so painful he had to use a cane. The old war injury had ended the captain's career in the navy and set him on the path of smuggling. Sometimes Nate suspected Drake was better at smuggling than following orders anyway.

"Your leg only hurts when you want it to," Nate said, stepping aside to let the two men in. "Usually when you need sympathy from attractive ladies."

"Speaking of attractive ladies." Drake's eyes lit upon Patience.

The color in her cheeks was near crimson. Drake removed his hand and gave a bow. "Miss Patience Grey, what a pleasure to see you in a gown."

Knight hovered near the doorway, his great hulk seeming to sap the light from the room. Women were usually intimidated by him but Patience seemed more disconcerted by Drake's flattery than the beast of a man.

"You know Mr. Knight, do you not?" Nate asked her.

"We have never been formally introduced," she said, purposefully ignoring Drake.

Knight gave a nod of his head and Nate imagined that was the man's idea of an introduction so he left it at that.

"Where is this lovely French belle then?" Drake asked.

"In the drawing room." Nate motioned to the door. "She is to remain in the house and guarded at all times. So far we have had no trouble but we cannot be sure that the information we need is where she said it is and I certainly do not trust her to stay."

Drake grinned. "There's nothing I like more than watching a woman's every move. You can rely on us to guard her."

"As long as that is all you do," Nate warned. If Nate himself had a reputation for enjoying ladies' company, Drake was one hundred times worse. But he would not betray his duty for the sake of a woman, Nate knew that much.

"Stop fussing like an old woman and get to that dinner party," Drake ordered. "We can handle one woman between us, can't we, Knight?"

Knight gave a grunt of acknowledgement.

Nate glanced at the clock in the hallway. "Mrs. Rowley is around somewhere. She can feed and water you. We're late, we'd better make haste."

Drake near kicked them out of the house. Too keen to meet Pauline, he reckoned. But still, they needed someone to watch over her, just until they knew they had the information and he could not think of anyone else he trusted more than them, save from his brother.

They made their way down the steps and Patience let out a tiny squeak as her delicate slipper skidded on the wet steps. Nate caught her before she could tumble and she gripped his arms. Her fingers dug in through the fabric of his coat and he winced. Too damned strong for a girl.

"These shoes are too big," she muttered as she straightened herself.

Nate offered her an arm and escorted her down the rest of the steps. "Did you borrow those from Pauline?"

"Yes. I suppose I should be ashamed that a homeless, countryless woman has more clothing than I do."

Nate shrugged. "Some women are preoccupied with clothes, while others are...are well..."

"Preoccupied with competing with their brothers?" she suggested.

He chuckled. "And I think trying to best one's brothers is more important than clothing."

The carriage he had ordered for the occasion awaited them at the end of the steps. Rain dripped from the driver's coat and hat. He gave them a sour look. "I've been 'ere 'alf an hour already."

"And you can charge me extra for that half an hour," Nate offered.

The man's grumpy countenance changed swiftly and he straightened in his seat. "We'd best be off then."

Nate aided Patience into the carriage and the vehicle set off before he had even managed to sit down. He tumbled onto the seat opposite her. Once he had settled more comfortably he bit back a groan of regret. The lit lanterns on the side of the carriage warmed the inside of the vehicle enough so that he could fully admire Patience.

It was not as though he did not like admiring her but he certainly did not need the distraction. Every time they hit a rut—and that seemed to be every second—her breasts moved against the confines of that blasted dress.

He drew in a breath and forced his gaze to the spot behind her head. There was nothing of note there but at least there were no breasts to ogle.

"Knight is quite the brutish sort of man, is he not?"

Nate nodded. Knight. Yes, that was the sort of topic he could talk on. There was nothing remotely attractive or appealing about that man.

"He's a tough fellow. Good to have on one's side."

"And you met him through your brother?"

"Yes. Red brought him on board to help. He's the face of the operation. It's useful to have someone intimidating—means no one will ask questions."

"Even if they did, I doubt anyone would ever suspect you or your brother of being involved. As for Drake..."

"Yes, he's a scoundrel, but a good scoundrel." He chuckled. "He's *our* scoundrel I suppose is what I should say."

"That's one way to put it." She leaned forward and Nate bit back a groan. "So how do we get into Sir Magnus' library?"

Forcing his gaze from her cleavage, he looked into her eyes. "Perhaps you can use your feminine charms?"

Patience snorted. "We would be more likely to succeed using yours."

Chapter Seventeen

"Well that was a thorough waste of time." Patience grimaced at the cold, damp evening. Their carriage was nowhere to be seen. Apparently their driver was still annoyed at them for being late to depart and had decided to teach them a lesson. "I cannot believe I wore a dress for that."

Nate peered up and down the road. "If it's of any comfort, you looked beautiful."

Patience opened her mouth and closed it.

"You still do, even with your hair wilting in the rain."

She gave his arm a tap. "I have never been beautiful—you do not need to flatter me."

"I do not need to, but I wish to."

Nate should have bit his tongue in half to stop himself but he could not. Now was not the time for flattery or flirtation. They had wasted an entire evening listening to Magnus and his friends talk of business and society, and only the one mention of Pauline. Magnus had confided that he had tired of her and was on the lookout for another lady but the more time spent in Magnus' company, the more Nate was convinced that Magnus was not interested in a mistress at all and was simply using them as a cover for his true tastes.

The warm glow of lanterns drew his attention to the inn nearby. He motioned to it. "Let us wait in there. I have little intention of returning to the dinner party." He paused. "Besides, it might do to wait."

Patience peered at him. "You're plotting."

"Yes." He grinned and led her across the road to the inn. "Yes. We shall wait. And once Magnus is abed, we shall sneak into his house and find that information."

"You want to break into his house?"

"Why not?"

Patience shook her head in disbelief. "Well, it is better than attending any more dinner parties, I shall give you that."

Nate managed to find them a seat near the window. If he leaned around and peered through the murky glass, he could see the lanterns lit in the lower windows of Magnus' house. With any luck they could wait until he was asleep and slip in somehow.

Thankfully the inn was quiet with only a few travelers stopping in briefly. Nate nursed an ale while Patience sipped on some wine that made her curl up her nose and look far too adorable.

Adorable. Listen to him. He sounded like a little girl eyeing up a litter of puppies.

They waited over two hours. Patience kept suppressing yawns and the innkeeper kept eyeing them with annoyance, considering they had nursed the same drinks the entire time. Nate was tempted to order another but they had drunk wine and brandy at Magnus' and he wanted his head to remain clear. If someone put another ale in front of him, it was very likely he'd drink the whole damned thing.

"Nate," Patience hissed excitedly. "The lights are out."

He peered out of the window and nodded. "They are. But we had better wait a while longer to ensure he is abed and the servants aren't around."

Patience scowled but nodded. The damned woman was certainly keen to get involved in illegal activity. Any other woman would be running to the hills but here was Patience ready to hitch up her skirts and break down doors.

He grinned at the mental image and drained his ale, deciding the last drop would not hurt. He placed a coin on the table in the hopes of making up for not drinking enough for the innkeeper's liking and motioned for Patience to follow.

They made their way across the road and up the side of the house. Nate tested one of the cellar windows to no avail. The door that led into the back of the house was no good either. Completely shadowed in dark, the rear of the building offered no other ways to enter.

Nate stilled when something rustled nearby. Patience smacked into his back with an *oof.*

"Shh," he said.

"A fox or something," she said. "Come on, let us try there." She motioned to the window on the second floor that he had been ignoring. It was slightly ajar but would need to be forced open.

"Too high."

"I can climb. Just give me a boost up."

He shook his head again but she was already making her way over to the window. She eyed the drainpipe that ran up the side of the building then bent to twist her skirts up. She tied them in a bunch around her thighs.

"Pauline is not going to be impressed," he hissed.

Patience waved away his words and nodded to the corner of the pipe where it hooked onto the wall. "Lift me up and I can climb from there."

Nate sighed. There was no fighting her on this and he couldn't think of any other way of getting in. If he climbed the pipe, it would likely give way under his weight. He only hoped nothing happened to Patience or he would never forgive himself.

Nor would her brothers. He'd be lucky to retain his balls if he let her come to harm.

He bent and lifted her up onto one shoulder. From there she hooked her arms around the pipe and one foot into the wall-attachment. He grimaced as metal creaked but there was no crash as the pipes gave way or thud as Patience fell. Instead she made her way up the pipe with the ease of a young boy climbing a tree and reached over to ease open the window.

His heart remained in his mouth the entire time as she leaned out to pull it open. After three tries, he was ready to call this whole debacle off but the window finally popped open. She shimmied in and vanished.

Nate had to resist the desire to pace. What if someone caught her? What if she got hurt?

"Nate."

He peered up to see Patience leaning out of the window. She threw something down to him and it took him a moment to realize she'd flung down a silken rope. He scowled and tugged on it. It felt secure but where the devil had she found a rope?

"If I fall on my arse, I'll throttle her," he muttered, before using the rope to pull himself up to the window.

Patience helped haul him in and he paused once he was on his feet to gather his breath.

"Where the hell did you find this?" He lifted the rope.

"From the bed." She motioned to the heavy curtains around it and he noted several other long lengths of silk rope holding back the fabric. Patience had tied two together and looped it around the heavy bed.

"A fine job I'm not heavier."

"I knew it would hold you," she whispered.

"A good thing this wasn't Magnus' room either," he grumbled.

"Just because I could climb up and you could not does not mean you need to be grumpy with me." She grabbed his hand. "Come, let us find the documents and be gone before we are found."

He nodded and used the grip on her hand to force her back behind him. He was done with watching Patience take risks. "I'll take the lead."

She rolled her eyes but complied. Nate eased open the bedroom door and peered up and down the dark hallway. They slipped out, observed only by the portraits of ancient and not-so-ancient ancestors. Nate had already visited the library twice for brandy so he knew the way well enough, even if it was not so easy to find in the dark. He led Patience downstairs and through the drawing room. The embers in the fire still lingered, and for that he uttered up a prayer of thanks. It meant navigating the room that was crowded with furniture was not too difficult.

He opened one door, then closed it, realizing his mistake. "This one."

Motioning to the other door, he hastened over, Patience still in hand. Keen to get to the shadows of the library, they slipped in swiftly and she shut the door with caution.

For a townhouse, Magnus' abode boasted a decent sized library. Bookshelves touched the ceilings and the room occupied nearly half of the ground floor. A large window at one end released a gentle glow from the lit lanterns outside and the fire had not been put out in here either so it was not too hard to find their way around. How easy it would be to find the book, however, was another matter.

"Voltaire," he reminded Patience.

She peered up at the books. "Where do we start?"

"Maybe they are alphabetized."

She moved to the first bookcase and peered at the title. "No, it looks like it might be by subject matter." She traced the spine of one of the books with a finger. "This looks to be the geography section."

"He must have a fiction section somewhere."

"You start there." She pointed to the opposite wall. "We'll meet in the middle."

Nate nodded and squinted at the titles in the first book case. "History," he murmured.

"Philosophy here."

He scanned several more titles and moved onto the next bookcase. The man had far too much non-fiction if you asked him. Where were all the exciting tales of action and adventure? Although, after tonight, he did not know if he wanted any more action and adventures. A relaxing cup of tea would be nice. He glanced at Patience. With a wonderful woman at his side, perhaps?

He shook his head. Age really was catching up with him.

"Nate," she hissed. "Over here."

He hurried over. She motioned to the books. "Look, Chaucer, Defoe...oh *Gulliver's Travels*. They're not in alphabetical order though."

Grimacing, he nodded. "You start at the bottom." On tiptoes, he scanned the titles. He must have looked at fifty or so before Patience let out a squeak.

"Shh."

"I've found it." She pulled out the book and stood.

He yanked open the bound leather and let the air in his lungs release.

"It's the documents, is it not?" she asked, pressing herself against him in anticipation.

"I think so." He pulled out the first letter—orders, he suspected, and a list of French names. The second was a map. "This must be it. Pauline wasn't lying."

"Come on, just take the book and we can check the rest later."

"Let us slip out the rear door. I don't much fancy any more climbing for the day."

"Coward." She jabbed him with an elbow.

"Ow." Nate rubbed his ribs. "It's more to do with not wishing to see you climb again. It was the most terrifying thing I have ever witnessed."

"Why should me climbing be terrifying?"

"Because I thought you were going to break your neck," he declared. "I do not know what I would have done if you had."

"Oh."

At that moment, he wished for more light. Or for them to be elsewhere. To see her expression properly and understand fully what that one syllable had meant. Did she like that he cared for her welfare?

He took her hand again and tried not to marvel at how perfectly her fingers slipped into his. If there was ever a time not to marvel over such trivial things, it was certainly when one was breaking into a house like a thief.

Chapter Eighteen

Patience's stomach felt like it was churning with bees. Except perhaps that was not right because bees would be uncomfortable and this was more of a wonderful, buzzing feeling that made her limbs warm and her breathing quicken. Much of it was to do with the fact they were standing in a house, without the knowledge of the owner, having scaled a wall and found all the information they needed. A lot more of it was also to do with Nate holding her hand and telling her he would hate to see her come to harm.

Nate turned the handle on the library door and stilled. Patience scowled.

"What is it?"

He put a finger to his lips and she clamped her lips together. Easing the door open farther, they both leaned into the gap to listen. She wasn't sure what Nate heard but there was definitely footsteps coming their way. She peered around the library. There were nooks and crannies covered in shadow but nowhere to hide two people.

Someone giggled. Then there was a deeper voice. Coming from the hallway, she suspected. Perhaps they would not come their way.

A door opened. Nate reacted before she could fathom what was happening. He tugged her out of the library and into the drawing room. Then he opened the door he had originally tried and shoved her into it. He followed her in and closed the door behind them.

Darkness swallowed her. She blinked into gloom to try to get her bearings. When she put out a hand, she felt something cold—

glass perhaps. If she felt the other way, there were more of the same objects. Wine bottles, she realized. This had to be the wine store.

She twisted into Nate. There was nothing cold here. Her hand landed on his chest and she felt the erratic beat of his heart. As her eyes adjusted to the darkness, she could make out the line of his shoulders and see the shelving around them. That was about it, however.

A door opened and the voices entered the room. Patience instantly recognized the baritone of Magnus but the giggle from the woman was not familiar. And she seemed to giggle a lot.

"Oh, sir." Another giggle.

Patience shifted and turned so that she could see through the crack in the door. Nate followed suit, pressing himself behind her so he could see over her head.

She blinked and peered harder.

"I'll be damned," Nate whispered.

She *did* recognize the woman in Magnus' arms. One of the serving girls. That was why he had not been interested in Pauline. He was indulging himself elsewhere and having a mistress was a cover.

The woman's work dress had been pushed down one shoulder. Magnus lavished kisses along her bare skin while fumbling his hand up under her skirts. Patience grew aware of the thudding of her heart picking up speed. Her skin grew hot.

Magnus broke away from the woman and moved out of Patience's view. It was wicked of her, but she was disappointed. She should not, but she wanted to see more.

When Magnus returned to the woman with a glass of brandy, Patience realized how close they were to being spotted. What if he decided to get a bottle of wine?

Her fears faded when the woman drained the brandy and cast the glass aside before taking Magnus into her arms. Her face a picture of ecstasy, Magnus kissed his way down her neck and back up. His hands began roaming once more, first pressing against her breasts, then down to bunch up her skirts. He pressed his hand underneath the layers and the maid released a moan.

"I have been waiting all evening for this," Magnus said against her cheek.

"Well, you insist on hosting dinner parties all the time."

"I have to keep up appearances."

"By having a mistress too?" the maid demanded, pulling back for a moment.

"She's gone now, you know that. I sent her on her way. There is no one else but you for me." He moved his hand against the woman's thighs and her eyes fluttered closed and she tilted her head back.

Whether what he said was true, Patience thought, she did not know, but the maid did not seem to mind.

Behind her, Nate grew fidgety. His body pressed into hers, his chest hard and unrelenting and his heart beating fiercely against her back. The same discomfort was beginning to envelop her. She wanted to writhe against him.

And that was when she understood...Nate was aroused. His erection lay hard against her back. She moved into it slightly, to be sure, and a barely audible groan escaped him. The spectacle in front of her began to lose its appeal. She turned to face him with barely an inch separating them.

The darkness had not eased. She still only saw his outline but it was enough. She heard his heavy breaths and knew he was feeling as she was. One of his hands came up to cup her cheek. The sudden, sweet warmth of it startled her and she had to bite her lip to prevent herself from making a sound.

She skimmed both hands up his arms, reveling in the taut, strong feel of his muscles underneath his dinner jacket. She let them rest on his upper arms and felt the muscles flex as he reached with his other hand to pull her firm against him.

Her heart pounded like cannon fire in her ears. Somewhere in the distance were the grunts and cries of lovemaking but she could hardly pay them any attention, not when she was flat against Nate, practically sightless and able to feel. Every. Little. Thing.

From the heat of his breath to the warmth of his palm, she felt it all. It was unlike anything she had ever experienced before.

"Patience," he murmured.

Patience. Even the way he said her name made her shudder with pleasure. If she thought it could not get any better, he brought his lips to hers. In the dark, she had been unable to predict the movement and the fission it sent down her spine, all the way to her borrowed slippers, made her tremble in his arms.

Lips slightly parted, she let him take the lead as he moved his soft, warm mouth over hers. Every inch of her tingled and her nipples pressed hard against her stays in protest of their confinement. She moved into him, rubbing herself against him in a bid to gain some relief.

A rumbling sound rose from his throat and he pressed the kiss harder, this time slipping his tongue into her mouth. She met his tongue with her own and trembled again. He kissed her over and over, deeper and harder. All she could do was take the onslaught and surrender herself to the sensations pouring over her. Lord Nathaniel Kingsley was kissing her. Her! Patience Grey, the strange girl who wore breeches.

A large cry from outside followed by a groan broke the moment. Nate drew away, his breaths heavy. He kept her close while they both sucked in gulps of air in the warm storage cupboard. Perspiration clung to her skin.

Nate peered out of the gap in the door but she did not try to turn. She waited, flat against him, taking in everything that had just happened. After a while there was the sound of a door closing and she heard a muffled declaration of Magnus taking the maid to bed. They waited a while longer before Nate opened the door and took her hand once more.

He escorted them silently through the house and slipped out of the rear door and into the gardens. The rope remained swinging from the window and if she'd thought about it, she would have taken it down but even if Magnus noticed, they had taken nothing of importance—at least not to his knowledge.

Once they were well away from the house, Nate paused and took Patience in his arms. He kissed her on the lips once.

"We did it."

"Yes, we did," she agreed, picking up on Nate's infectious grin.

The carriage had obviously never tried to come for them as they did not spot it on their journey home. Thankfully the walk was not hard, even in her borrowed slippers, and the rain had eased off to a light drizzle. Her hair had likely been ruined by their encounter in the wine store so at least she had an excuse for her unseemly state.

Hand in hand they made their way to the house. The excitement swirling in her stomach had yet to abate and she did not think it would for a long while yet. They had completed their mission and Nathaniel Kingsley had kissed her. She could not say what that meant but she had little inclination to study it at present. For the time being she was going to enjoy the memory of a time she had reveled in being a woman.

Lamps still glowed in the windows of the house. Nate's friends had likely opted to remain up to watch over Pauline until their return. Joyce was up still too as she opened the door and began tutting over their damp state.

"Those drivers are terrible. They are so impatient," she said. "They'll never wait for anyone. Let me take your coats." She held out her hands as they unbuttoned their coats. "Oh, we have more visitors! Your brother, Miss Patience!"

Patience scowled. "Jacob?"

"Yes, that's the one." Joyce smiled. "He said you would be surprised to see him."

"I am, I thought he would still be abed, nursing his leg."

"Well, he looks in fine health to me," Joyce said.

What was Jacob doing here? Patience handed her pelisse to Joyce and strode into the drawing room. Sure enough, her brother sat next to Pauline, his leg propped up on a footstool with a cup of tea in hand. Knight and Drake stood near the fireplace, both looking as though they were still on guard.

He grinned when he saw her. "Patience! Christ, you're wearing a dress."

"Yes, Jacob, I am," she said tightly. "What are you doing here? Should you not be resting?"

"Well, the doctor said I was recovered enough to begin walking about again. Said the exercise would do me good."

"I am certain he likely meant a stroll down to the harbor, and not a trip to Falmouth."

Nate entered the room, the book still clutched in his hand. Pauline smiled when she saw it.

"You found the book then," she asked. "And with everything in it. See I was not lying."

"Yes, we have it," Nate said.

"Excellent news." Her brother eased himself up and limped over. "May I?"

Nate handed over the book, albeit reluctantly. Patience felt the same. This was their discovery, their work. She did not much feel like giving it to her brother.

Jacob leafed through the information, his expression growing more excited by the moment. "Perfect, perfect." He murmured. "Well, the good news is, I have come to rescue you."

"Recuse me?" Patience asked.

"Yes. You can all return home. Pauline has agreed to accompany me to Truro. From there we shall be setting her up with some protection and I shall get this information taken to London."

Patience glanced at Pauline who rolled her eyes. Somehow she suspected Pauline would not need protection. The woman had more wit than most men put together.

"You did not need to come," Patience protested. "We had it all in hand."

"As I can see." Jacob clapped Nate on the back. "You did a fine job of looking after my little sister, even if she is a little damp. Excellent gown, though. You almost look like a lady, Patience."

She gave him a hard, long glare then swiveled on her toes. "I am going upstairs to change."

Slamming the door shut behind her, she heard her brother ask Nate what on earth he had done wrong.

Everything, she thought as she stomped upstairs. He had come to steal her moment. He had teased her in front of everyone. He had assumed Nate had done all the work. None of them would ever see her as more than the tiny, silly, Patience Grey who could do nothing without the help of a man. She swiped away a tear of frustration and slammed the bedroom door shut.

Chapter Nineteen

Patience hardly knew what to say to Nate on the journey home. What could she say? *Sorry you were dragged into this and wasted your time while my brother gets to take all the credit? Actually, I quite enjoyed your company after all? And perhaps I was wrong and you're not such a bad man after all? Would you like to spend more time with me?*

She shook her head. No, there was nothing more to be said so she remained quiet while the carriage rolled across the bumpy road that ran along the coastline.

Drake appeared disappointed to leave Falmouth. Perhaps more because he did not wish to leave Pauline. The handsome captain had perfected a sort of masculine sulk ever since they had packed up and departed. Patience had to admit to being quite intrigued by Pauline's effect on men. It was certainly something to behold.

She could not deny being envious of Pauline and how comfortable she was using her womanly wiles to get through life. Not that Patience wanted to use what little wiles she had or was even interested in affecting men but to be so comfortable in one's own body was quite something.

If Knight was disappointed to leave without completing the mission, he did not reveal it. Eyes closed, arms folded, he remained perfectly still, even as the carriage tossed them about like toy dolls being played with by a child. The man was like a rock that neither weather nor time could move.

Patience tilted her head and eyed his scarred face. She knew little of Mr. Lewis Knight even though he had been living in Penshallow for several years. She did not even know where he resided. Most of the time he could be found in the Ship Inn which was out of bounds for a woman like her. Some of the women said he was a criminal, on the run from the law, but surely not. Nate had said nothing of a criminal past even if what they were doing now was not exactly legal.

The carriage hit a particularly big rut and Nate's shoulder bumped into hers. "Forgive me," he murmured.

Their gazes connected and Patience was sure her heart nearly jumped from her throat. His blue eyes were a little darker than usual, probably because of the gloomy confines of the carriage. Either way, they seemed to reach deep down inside her and twist her stomach into a tangle of knots. If she looked hard enough, she was certain there was an unspoken message there.

What it was, however, she did not know. If only she was like Pauline and understood men. For all her time trying to pretend to be one, she still had little idea how they actually thought—particularly one like Nate, who was far more complex than his arrogant exterior would have one believe.

She looked away, her cheeks hot, and focused on peering through the clouded and slightly mud-splattered window.

"I have asked my driver to stop at your house first."

Forced to look at him again, she nodded. "Excellent."

A pang of dread speared her stomach. The house would be empty apart from her mother who had likely hardly noticed she was gone. Her moment of excitement and adventure was over. Now what would she do?

Never before had she longed for a journey to take more time or for something like a broken wheel to befall them. Unfortunately, nothing delayed them and they arrived outside her house by mid-afternoon. Knight peeled his eyes open long enough to nod his farewell whilst Drake gave her a grin and a wink and told her he hoped he would see her again soon.

Patience hardly knew how to respond to his flirtatious manner that seemed to be his default so she merely smiled before taking Nate's proffered hand and exiting the carriage.

As her foot hit the shingled path in front of the house, the front door opened. She had to take a moment to comprehend who the man standing upon the doorstep was.

"Harry!"

Her eldest brother, and the head of the family, beamed at her and rushed down the steps to greet her. Nate stepped back so that Harry could embrace her. Patience found herself enveloped in her brother's hold, barely able to breathe but far too happy to complain about it.

He finally stepped back and she craned her neck to view him. War had aged him a little, making the creases along his forehead deeper and peppering his hair with strands of white. Other than that, he looked in good health and the same as he had always been.

"When did you return?" she demanded.

"Only two days ago. I'm to remain for two months and likely head back out to Spain after that."

Her heart dropped a little but it was nothing new. Her brother had been coming and going out of her life ever since he got his commission. At least they would have a little time together.

Harry turned his attention to Nate and offered out a hand. "Nate, it has been a while. I hear I am to offer my congratulations."

Nate took her brother's hand and threw her a puzzled look. "Uh..."

"Mother told me all about it," he explained to Patience. "If we hurry things along, we can have you wed before I leave. There's nothing I would like more than to see my sister taken care of."

Patience peered at Harry for a moment. What on earth had her mother said? She knew Patience wasn't going to marry anyone, let alone Nate.

"Everyone is very happy for you, Patience." Harry grinned. "Of course a few were surprised. I did not even know you two were friends."

"Well, it was very sudden," she found herself saying.

"All that matters is that you are happy."

She gulped. Never had her brother looked so proud of her, so pleased and happy. Had it been plaguing him that his sister was not taken care of by another man?

"Um, yes. I am."

Nate lifted his eyebrows but said nothing.

"You must be weary. Will you come in for a moment, Nate? We have a lot to discuss."

Nate shook his head. "I had better return home." He motioned to the carriage where Drake was peering out, trying his best to appear like he was not listening at all. "I am not alone. But I shall call on Patience tomorrow if I have your permission, Harry? Then we can discuss things fully." He gave Patience a pointed look.

She grimaced inwardly. Who knew how her brother had come up with the idea they were truly engaged but for the life of her she could not bring herself to correct him, not when he appeared so happy. She would put him to rights, of course. Just not yet.

Not yet.

Not whilst he was beaming at her. Apparently the only thing she ever needed to do to win her brother's pride was to get married.

Nate bid them farewell and she stood by her brother's side to watch the carriage depart. When Nate returned tomorrow, she would let him know that she would rectify this. She certainly wouldn't hold him to a marriage that had been intended as nothing more than a cover. Or that anyone aside from a select few were meant to know about.

"Harry, when you say everyone is happy for me, what did you mean?"

He grinned. "The whole village is talking of it. I think they are likely as surprised as me but they say if anyone can tame Lord Nathaniel Kingsley, it is you."

She sighed. "I am not at all sure he is tamable."

Her brother paused on the first step into the house. "Patience, are you happy? Did he treat you well during your time away? Mother said you were doing something of great importance but could tell me little."

"Where is mother anyway?"

"In the drawing room, of course."

"Of course." She put a hand to Harry's arm. "It is good to have you home. All is well, I promise. Now, I must speak with mother."

She strode into the house, eased open the door to the drawing room and closed it gently behind her. Her mother sat as though she had never moved from her position by the window, except now she was painting something else—a hare by the looks of it, set against lush green grass.

"Mama." She approached slowly, aware that if she jolted her mother out of 'the moment' as she liked to call it, she would not get a word of sense.

Her mother held up a finger then pressed it to pursed lips while studying the bare bones of her painting. Shades of brown and green stained her fingertips and apron and there were a few streaks upon her cheeks. Her hair was ruffled and wild and Patience detected a few paint-tinged strands.

Finally, her mother turned her attention to Patience. She lowered the brush into a jar on the windowsill and smiled. "All done then?" She opened her arms for an embrace.

Patience nodded and bent to hug her mother. "All done. Did Jacob tell you he was to join me in Falmouth?"

"He mentioned something. I thought he needed more time to rest but he said he could hobble about. He missed Harry's arrival home, unfortunately."

"Yes, it seems he could manage," Patience said, biting back a sigh. If only he had waited a little longer. They could have finished the mission themselves and explained to Harry that she was never really engaged to Nate.

Patience drew over a chair and sat it next to her mother's. Slinging both legs over it, she rested her arms upon the back and fixed her mother with a look. "Mama, did you tell Harry I was engaged to Nathaniel Kingsley?"

She blinked at her. "Well, you are, are you not?"

"No, of course not." Patience pinched the bridge of her nose. "Mama, it was pretend, remember?"

A crease appeared between her mother's brows. "Was it?"

"Yes. It was a cover."

Mama tilted her head. "Are you sure? You look so much like a woman in love?"

"Of course I am sure."

Her mother shrugged, sending her lace shawl slipping from her shoulders. Patience stood and helped her readjust it. Mama patted her hand.

"He's a handsome man and a little wild. I think I like that for you. Better than some staid old grump who would stick you in silk and feathers."

Patience laughed. "I do not think I would let any man stick me in silk and feathers, though I did wear a dress twice."

"Oh indeed? Did you like it?"

"Once perhaps." A touch of warmth spread into her cheeks at the memory of how Nate had looked at her. For the first time in her life she had understood a little of what Pauline experienced every day. There was power in femininity. Being a woman did not always have to mean being weak.

Her mother peered up at her. "Are you sure you are not in love?"

"Very sure, Mama. How could I be? I hardly know the man."

"What a shame. He is so very handsome."

"You know handsome is not enough for me."

"That I do. Shall you tell your brother? He was quite happy to hear you had an offer. You know how these men worry about us looking after ourselves."

"I shall tell him soon," Patience vowed.

She just had to find a way to break the news without disappointing Harry. He had looked after them all since he was five and ten. It was quite an undertaking with four brothers and one sister. The last thing she wanted to do was upset him, but she could hardly hold Nate to a fake marriage, could she?

No.

She gave her mother a kiss on the cheek. "I am going to wash and change. Please do not say anything more to Harry. I shall solve this problem."

"It is only a problem if you make it one, dear."

Patience shook her head and left her mother to her painting. How she could think that an engagement that was not really an engagement was not a problem, she did not know. Of course there was the issue that the whole village seemed to think they were to be wed too. She would have to get Nate to call it off, so to speak. Certainly, she would be pitied by everyone and in some eyes, ruined, but she had never cared much for the idea of marriage and her suitors were hardly lining up at the door to propose. Let Nate save his pride and break things off—that was the best way of dealing with it.

She just hoped Harry did not take offense and feel the need to call him out.

Patience paused outside the drawing room and pressed her back against the door. Oh what a pickle this was.

Chapter Twenty

"Little as I do not wish to interfere in your life—"

"Since when?" Nate snapped, folding away the newspaper and glaring at his brother over the breakfast table.

"I am not at all sure where you got this idea that I am determined to manage your every move."

Nate pushed aside his plate, unable to find his appetite and put the newspaper down beside it. "Because you always have."

"No." Red pointed a finger at him. "You think that I have. There's a difference between wanting to remain informed when your brother decides to go through with a faux engagement and managing your brother's life. Were I intent on managing it, I would have ridden to Falmouth and seen whether these rumors were true or not."

"Well, they're not, I can assure you of that. It was all a misunderstanding. What was meant to be a joke and a ruse has somehow turned into the real thing."

Red shook his head and sighed. "You shall have to get her to call it off. You cannot very well ruin the poor girl, especially when it is probably your fault the rumor started."

"How is it my fault?"

"Someone must have overheard you joking about it."

Damn, it was not the first time his actions had come back to bite him on the arse and it would not be the last no doubt.

"I'm to visit with Patience and her brother today. I shall ensure she wishes to break it off then inform Harry that, alas, his sister does not think I am good enough for her and that will be that."

"You're not," Red muttered, "but does she believe that?"

"Patience does not want to get married, let alone to me, I promise you that."

Taking a slow sip of his coffee, Red nodded. "I hope you are right."

"Anyway, what do you mean I'm not good enough for her? You're my brother, you should be singing my praises."

"You're a flirt and a rake. Not to mention a smuggler."

"As are you," Nate pointed out.

"As if I could forget. But I am not a rake."

"Only since you met Hannah. Now you think yourself some paragon of virtue."

A smile crossed his brother's face. It was a soft one—one that he had never seen before Hannah had entered their life. "Hannah did change me somewhat, yes."

"Should you not be worrying about your own wedding plans, anyway? Get your nose out of mine and concentrate on your own."

Red's brows lifted. "So there are wedding plans?"

"No, damn it. You know what I mean."

"Well, today I am to take Hannah to town." He waved a hand. "Dress fittings or something, I forget. Her father will be coming to town in a week which means we have little time to ensure the last haul is distributed."

"When do we go out again?"

"The wedding is in just under three weeks so once we've honeymooned, I plan to send the ship out again."

Nate nodded. "Excellent. I may accompany them. Wait for all the gossip to die down."

And a trip over to France combined with some hard work would clear his head of all this Patience nonsense.

Patience.

Damn it.

In spite of the drama from yesterday, he was itching to see her again. It was odd to sleep in his bed once more, knowing he would not wake up to see her face at breakfast. Not being able to end the evening cuddled under a blanket and whiling away the hours was somewhat disappointing too. Regardless of what happened after this blasted mistake was put to bed, he hoped they could remain friends.

He scowled to himself. Friends? With a woman? He searched his memory for some similar incident but could not recall one. Certainly he was on good terms with many of his conquests but they had never been friends.

"I had better get going." He stood and pushed back the chair. "If I do not quell this marriage nonsense, the townsfolk will have me hitched to her before sundown."

"There are worse fates," his brother muttered, hardly looking up from the letter next to his plate.

Worse fates than being married to Patience? Perhaps. But, Christ, the woman could drive a man to an early grave. It was all very well spending time with her when he knew it was going to end but to be chained to her forever.

He paused on his way out of the hallway. The inevitable shudder of dread did not finger its way down his spine. The chill that usually overtook him at the very idea of being in the matrimonial state refused to take hold. In fact he felt...well, perfectly normal. Happy even. A little excited at the idea of seeing Patience.

God Almighty, what the deuce was wrong with him? He'd have to see a doctor if this continued.

Nate opted to ride to Patience's house. The short journey hardly warranted having the carriage made ready and he could do with a bracing ride to clear the fatigue from his head. After a night of tossing and turning in his own bed, he could barely keep his eyes open.

He would need his wits about him today, however. Why the devil did she not deny their engagement to her brother?

Though, of course, he understood somewhat. From all Patience had told him, he knew how much she adored and admired Harry. He had appeared truly happy that she had found someone. But, as happy as her brother may be, that someone could not be Nate.

Nate made his way to the stables and was nearly toppled by the sheep racing toward him. He took the brunt of the collision on his shins and grunted.

"Good morning, sheep."

The sheep gave him a nudge which tended to mean she was happy to see him.

"Sorry, my lord, she's been trying to escape all week." A stable hand paused to bend double and suck in a breath.

Nate waved away his apology. "Not to worry, I shall see her back to her pen." He motioned to the sheep. "Come on, girl. Let's get you some breakfast."

The sheep followed obligingly. At least she now remained in her pen. It was only when he did not visit did she try to escape and get into the house to look for him. For the first weeks of their acquaintance she must have snuck her way into the house a dozen times. The housekeeper was none to happy about the sheep droppings she left on the ancient and expensive carpets.

He fed and fussed over the animal whilst his horse was saddled. She gave him a mournful look as he stood. "I'll be back soon, girl. With a name for you too if I can help it. Though what the devil you call a sheep I do not know."

Nate followed the main path out of his brother's estate. Tucked back from the village and nestled between hills, the house did not receive the full brunt of being by the ocean. It wasn't until one had ridden out from the gatehouse and along the road that cut along one side of the valley did one know they were by the seaside. Sea salt filled the air, brought in on a breeze that whipped the collar of his coat and threatened to turn into something more aggressive. He welcomed the cool bite of it on his skin.

The estuary meandered beside him, drained at present from low tide. Only mud flats and a tiny excuse for a river flowed past him but by evening it would be full and ready for boats. He met no one until he reached the outskirts of the village. A few greeted him normally but plenty of the villagers offered their congratulations. He nodded and thanked them all with a tight smile.

Apparently, they had all been hoping he would settle because many said as much. *About time*, said some. *First your brother, now you. We were all praying you would meet someone*, said the milliner. *Well done, congratulations, everyone is happy for you.* All the words rang in his head until he reached the steps of Patience's house. He tried to shake them away. The last thing he needed was expectation. He'd done his best to avoid it all his life.

A maid answered the door and led him into the drawing room. Though he had been inside the Greys' house before, it did not feel homely or welcoming as it had in the past. Patience's brother stood at the back of the room, his back rigid, hands clasped behind him, like an old Grandfather clock slowly counting each second. Patience must have been sitting on one of the sofas and had risen upon his entry. Today she wore buff pantaloons and a white shirt. He only briefly noted the curve of her breasts—very briefly—aware of her brother watching over him. The warm welcoming smile had departed. Had Patience told him already?

"Good morning, Harry. I was wondering if I might have a word with Patience?"

Her brother nodded slowly, a flicker of warning in his eyes. "Of course."

Patience watched her brother leave. Once he had exited the room, she went to the door that had been left ajar and closed it gently so that it did not make a sound as it shut. She turned to him, eyes lowered, hands clasped in front of her.

"I know I should have corrected him instantly."

"Yes."

"I will rectify this. I just was so excited to see him and he seemed so thrilled for me."

Harry did not seem quite as thrilled now but there was no sense in wondering why. The chances were Harry had mulled over it and realized a rogue like himself was not good enough for his sister. He ran his gaze over her features, so downcast and guilt-ridden. Despite her melancholy, it pleased him to see her. He had missed those full lips, so often pulled into a mutinous pout, and those flashing eyes that were usually fired up with anger at him, because, of course, he always managed to rile her.

And, good God, did he enjoy riling her. Never had he had so much fun exchanging wits with a woman.

She had continued to adopt a softer hairstyle too. Though not as neat as one might expect, the wild curls about her face and piled atop her head made him want to thrust his fingers into them and pull her in for a kiss.

His groin tightened making him realize it had been too long since he'd kissed her. Too long, but perhaps not long enough. There wasn't enough time for him to forget the warmth of her mouth and her eager, inexperienced passion. Not enough time for him to put it to the back of his mind and remind himself that it had been one kiss and they were not engaged—not really. There would not be a repeat.

"I believe," Nate started, "that it may have been my fault we are in this pickle. Likely someone overheard me jesting with my brother. So we are both to blame here."

She opened her mouth then closed it. Moving around the sofa, she ran a finger across the carved wooden back before looping around and coming back to stand in front of him. He had to admit to spending most of those several precious seconds watching her arse and hips move in delightful ways.

"You must call it off," she finally declared. "Call it off and this shall all be over."

Nate frowned. "I cannot."

"But you must."

He shook his head. "No, *you* must call it off."

"I will not," she declared, that flashing in her eyes that he had been so fond of warning him he was in for trouble. Perhaps he did not miss that as much as he had thought.

"Why not? We have to put a stop to this somehow."

"My brother will be so upset with me that I turned you down. I'm sure you are aware that I am not flooded with offers."

"If I end things with you, you shall be ruined. No man will go near you again."

She waved a hand. "Yes, yes, I shall be tainted goods." She uttered the last word with distaste. "But I have no plans to marry, no eager suitors that shall be put off. You must be the one to end it."

"If you end it, little one, there shall be no scandal. The banns have not been read, you would be well within your rights to call it off, and no one would think any less of you."

"A woman is within her rights to change her mind, of course, but I know many who would think less of me. Why would a woman like me turn down a man like you?" She jabbed a finger against his chest. "*You* must do it. No one will question why. They will simply think you had a moment of madness and now you have awoken from it."

He snatched that finger and held her captive by that one digit. He tugged her close, using that small hold. They were nearly toe to toe by the time he was done with her.

"Your brother will call me out."

"He will not, I swear it. I will make sure of it."

"I'm not doing it."

"Well, nor am I."

"You must eventually. Much longer and the entire village shall be planning our wedding."

Her chin jutted out. "You do it."

Her breath whispered over his face, hot and erratic. His whole body tightened. He searched those blazing eyes. "You. Damn. Well. Do it."

"Never."

Any thought of arguing vanished. He would wear her down once she realized he would not give in. But, for the moment, he had other things he needed to do. Namely, kiss her.

He brought his mouth down hard, trying to punish her perhaps, except it did not work. She met his kiss with equal force and latched her hands around his neck. A groan tore from the back of his throat. He bundled her into him, holding her tight against his arousal.

Somewhere, in the distance, a door latch clicked. He heard it but could not register it until someone coughed. He instantly released Patience and turned around.

Patience's mother grinned at them. "Oh dear."

He grimaced inwardly. Now he would never be able to call it off. The only way to stop this marriage was for Patience to end things. Somehow, he would have to persuade her. The only problem was, with his mind still seared from her kiss, he could not quite recall why it was such a terrible idea.

Chapter Twenty-One

The warmth of the Ship Inn barely touched the chill in Nate's bones. After an evening of distributing and hiding the goods, the encroaching winter weather had eaten deep inside. Red gave a shudder and tugged off his gloves to make the most of the heat that filled the old medieval building.

Nate ducked under a low beam and led the way to their usual spot, near the fire. The table and four chairs were empty. Everyone knew this was where they spent their time and with a man like Knight on their side, no one dare take their spot.

Knight opted for the chair by the window, always keen to be able to see what was happening in the room. Nate, Red, and Drake occupied the other chairs and Drake threw up a hand to motion to one of the barmaids. Knight took a moment to survey the room. Nate knew little about him—none of them did—but they all trusted him with their life. He worked harder than any of them and had been known to use his great size to get them out of sticky situations once or twice.

However, just because he trusted Knight it didn't mean Nate did not wonder about him. Why did he always look as though he was on guard? Who was he expecting to see? Unlike the rest of them, Knight had no cover. He was no nobleman nor a captain like Drake. Knight was the face of their smuggling ring and he did a perfect job of it. No one would dare hand him over or question his activities.

Louisa made her way over to their table, a tray of ale and whisky ready for them. She handed out the drinks and propped the tray under one arm. "Cold night?"

"The temperature is dropping," Drake agreed. "It will make life harder for the next few months."

"So long as we don't get damned snow, I'll be happy," said Red.

"If you're having trouble...um...moving things on, you know I have space here," Louisa offered.

It would not be the first time she had helped them. There had been a time or two when they'd needed to hide from the customs men or stow their goods elsewhere but they avoided bringing Louisa into their business as much as they could. The fact was that if either he or Red were found guilty of smuggling, they'd probably get a light tap on the wrists or have to pay a fine. The rest of their group would not be so lucky and they certainly did not want Louisa to pay the price for their activities.

Red shook his head. "There'll be no need for that. If the roads get blocked, we can manage."

"Well the offer is always there," she said with a smile.

Nate peered at Knight, only just realizing how quiet he was being. Which was not at all unusual but there was something in his manner that drew Nate's attention. He appeared more uncomfortable than normal in his huge body and... Nate stared harder...bloody hell, was the man blushing? Knight swung a quick look up at Louisa then cast his gaze quickly away. A smile quirked Nate's lips. The man with a heart of stone had a fancy for Louisa. Who would have thought it?

Louisa glanced around the room. "I hear there's a few broken-hearted girls in the village now."

Drake held up his hand. "It was not me. I did not touch them."

Laughing, Louisa shook her head. "I meant because both Kingsley men are now engaged. Funny, I never thought Patience Grey to be your type, Nate."

"Well, I—" She was right of course. Patience was not his type until, well, she had become his type. He was beginning to suspect she was now his only type.

"Oh, I had better dash. Rosie looks swamped." Louisa ducked away leaving Nate with the aftermath of her words and several stares from his friends.

"What is it?"

"You're still engaged?" Drake asked. "I thought you were going to have her call it off."

"I tried," he muttered. "The damned woman won't do it."

Red leaned in, cradling his whisky. "She won't do it? She wants to hold you to it. I did not take Patience for the sort to wrangle a marriage in a dishonest manner."

"No, it's not like that. She says it will disappoint her brother too much. She told me I have to be the one to call it off."

"Well why have you not?" his brother asked.

"Because it will ruin her. It's far better she call it off, you know that," Nate snapped.

Drake shrugged. "If she is willing to put up with the aftermath, you might as well call it off. At least it saves you some pride."

"I don't care about my pride."

The captain laughed. "Oh we know that. You would not have charmed half the population of Cornwall into bed, had you cared."

Nate shot him a look. "Says you, Captain Drake. You've bedded the other half."

A smug smile crossed his face. "And then some."

"I do not know why you two need to be in competition to bed the most number of women. You need to keep your cocks in your breeches and your heads in the game." Red leaned back and folded his arms. "You don't see Knight running off with a new woman every night."

"He must be a eunuch." Drake jabbed an elbow into Knight's side.

Knight grunted. "I bed women," he protested.

Nate eyed the man. He had never seen him with a woman and as far as he knew, Knight had zero ability to charm one. "Scaring women away with your scowl does not count as bedding them."

"Not all women fear me." Knight swung a glance past Nate and he was convinced it had to have been to look at Louisa. Christ, the man had it bad.

"Anyway, we were discussing Nate here and the wife he has somehow nearly gained," Drake said. "To be honest, she's a pretty thing. A little rough around the edges but those breeches she likes to wear." He made a noise in the back of his throat. "They cup her just..." He lifted both hands. "Not to mention those ti—"

Nate cut him off with a punch. Drake tumbled back, his chair toppling over and sending him to the floor. Before Nate could do anything else, Knight had stepped between them both leaving Nate nursing his sore knuckles.

Drake came to his feet and clutched his jaw with a grin. "I was only telling the truth."

Nate narrowed his gaze at the man and sucked in a long breath. He had never struck out at his friends—did not even consider himself to have a temper really. All he knew was that when Drake began talking about Patience like that, a red mist had descended. What was this woman doing to him?

Red put his hands out to either side and made a lowering motion. "Let us finish our drinks. Drake will watch his mouth and Nate will watch his fists."

Drake nodded. "I'll watch them carefully. Did not know you had it in you, Nate."

"Maybe it will knock your obsession with tits from you," Nate said through gritted teeth.

A laugh escaped Drake. "Never."

Nate could not help grin. "Was worth a try."

"Can we get back to our drinks?" Knight asked, motioning to the table.

Nodding, Nate sat and the rest followed suit. "I will not apologize." He directed this at Drake.

"I did not expect you to. Though you might want to think again about persuading Patience to call off the engagement. If she can make you lose your temper, she must be quite a woman." Drake picked up an ale, drained it and motioned for a second.

"She is. That does not mean I should marry her."

"Does it not?"

Nate eyed Knight. He tried not to be taken back by the brute's inference. "There are many women like Patience out there."

"Is there?" Knight's face remained expressionless.

"Yes, damn it." There had to be. Surely if he continued searching, remaining a bachelor and enjoying all the opposite sex could give him, he would find another woman like her?

"Are you certain?" the giant of a man pressed.

"Since when do you ask so many questions?" It had to be the most amount of words Nate had ever heard from the usually silent man. Why was everyone so bloody interested in his affairs suddenly?

"I think Knight's point is that we have never seen you quite so invested in a woman before," Red said. "You've certainly never been ready to kill a man over a woman before."

"I wouldn't have killed Drake," he grumbled.

"Not even if I mentioned her tits again?" Drake gave a flash of teeth.

Nate thrust a finger at the captain. "Never mention them ever again."

Drake threw up his hands. "See? He's as lost as you were when you met Hannah." He motioned to Red.

"I was not lost," his brother protested. "But, yes, Nate is in deep. Even if he does not know it yet."

Nate slammed down his jug of ale, making it slosh over the sides. "Goddamn it, stop talking about me like I'm not here."

Red fixed him with a serious look. "Face it, Nate. You never lose your temper over a woman and you are never grouchy. There is something about this woman, obviously. You could end this all with ease and yet you choose not to. Now you must decide if whatever this is is worth pursuing. God knows this bachelor act is getting old."

"You're technically still a bachelor," Nate pointed out.

"Not for much longer and I certainly never indulged in the lifestyle like you did." Red leaned in. "Think carefully, Nate. Do you have any interest in any other woman at present?"

"Well, no, but there's hardly a huge variety here."

"And if there was, would you want any of them over Patience?"

Nate paused and considered. The fact was that if Patience was in a room full of beauties all dressed up and primped to within an inch of their lives, he would only be interested in her. He was only interested in her.

And that had to mean something.

"I'll be damned," he muttered under his breath.

Red slapped him on the back. "Looks like your balls finally dropped. Welcome to the world of being a man."

The other men around the table laughed. Nate only felt numb. He'd never considered what would happen if he fell for a woman. Certainly he had held great admiration for many, and undoubtedly plenty of desire, but never anything like this.

He supposed there was only one thing for it. He would have to persuade Patience to make their engagement real.

Chapter Twenty-Two

"What are you doing here?" Patience asked as she fought to pull on her riding gloves.

"Is that any way to greet your fiancé?" Nate flashed a grin. It made her stomach turn itself inside out.

"You are not my fiancé," she protested.

"According to everyone else I am."

She sighed. "Nate, all you need to do is declare it was a mistake and we can end this."

His smile softened and there was something odd flickering in his blue eyes. A kind of softness that she had never witnessed before. "Come, the birds will not shoot themselves."

"How did you know I was going shooting?"

"Your brother mentioned as much yesterday."

"You know you could have used that moment to tell him the wedding was not going to happen." She continued fighting with her glove. She never had any problems with kid leather before but then she never normally had to wrestle with the things in front of the most handsome and charming man she had ever met.

"If you had listened to our conversation, you would have realized why that was not at all possible."

Scowling, she huffed at her wretched glove. Whatever they had talked about behind closed doors, her brother had told her nothing. She imagined it was the usual sort of thing—how much dowry she would bring and such like. It would be a paltry sum to a man like Nate. Which brought up the question yet again, why on earth did he not simply give in and announce it was all over?

Nate stepped forward, his boots clacking on the tiled floor of the hallway. He took the glove from her and eased it on before doing up the three buttons on the inside of her wrist. Then he snatched the other from where it was tucked under her arm and did the same. Once he was done, he swept a kiss across her lips.

All of it had her so taken aback that she was unable to react. Unless one counted standing frozen with one's mouth ajar as a reaction.

"My horse is waiting. I thought we could hunt on my brother's land, if you have no objection. It is certainly more suited to hunting than the woods."

Had she been in better charge of her senses, she would have declined. She hunted on a regular basis, on her own usually. She only took one gun and had no need for any aid. However, the shooting would be better on the Earl of Redmere's land.

But why was he doing this? There was no need. Did he think to persuade her to break it off? If he did, he was going about it the wrong way. She loved to ride and hunt, and there would be nothing better than doing it on estate land.

"I—"

"Excellent." He took her hand, gave her another kiss on the lips and helped her mount her horse before following suit.

Heat infused her cheeks the entire ride through the village. They crossed the bridge over the estuary and it seemed everyone was fascinated by them. If they were in doubt as to whether the rumors were true, they would not be now. What sort of a game was Nate playing?

Once they moved past the fishermen's cottages and the road widened, she came to his side. "You realize we shall be the talk of the town today?"

"Good."

"Good?"

"Yes. You deserve to be talked of."

She shook her head. "I have no idea what you mean but you know that will make calling things off all the more difficult."

"If you call it off, yes."

"You know I cannot. My brother will be furious."

"He will understand. That is, if that's really what you want."

"What I want? Of course it's..." She sucked in a breath. This man was confusing her. It was what he wanted, was it not? Surely it was? How could they get married? They might have lived around each other for years but they had not really come to know each other until recently, and a few kisses and conversations were not enough to make a marriage, were they?

Not to mention there was no chance Nate could really want her. Not truly. She was so far removed from marriage material, it was laughable.

They crossed under the gate that indicated the start of the earl's land. It stretched over a flat inlet of land that had been carved out of the valley when the estuary had been wider, likely many hundreds of years ago. The land extended up over the hills on which sheep and cattle were kept. Trees dotted the grass which was segmented off from the rest of the world by way of brick walls and a wooden fence. Smoke swirled from the gatehouse and lamps were lit in the windows.

They made their way up toward the fields behind the house and dismounted there. Patience tried her best to focus on the hunting but it was mightily distracting to be with Nate and she did not perform as well as she would have liked. Mostly she did not outperform Nate and that riled her.

After an hour of his company, she began to forget she was with the great Lord Nathaniel and as he teased and flirted, she relaxed. With several excellent shots under her belt, they called it a day.

"Would you mind if I check on the sheep?" he asked as they mounted their horses.

"Not at all."

They headed toward the outer stables where the farm animals were kept. The horses were allowed a moment to drink and eat while Nate opened the sheep's pen and gave her a pat on the head. The odd relationship between the two made her smile. Who would have thought a smuggling, roguish lord would care for a sheep? He glanced her way and the breath left her lungs. He gave her the same affectionate look that he bestowed upon the sheep.

Could he care for her too? No, surely not.

"Will you come in for some refreshments? My brother will not be at home. He is dealing with this wedding malarkey."

Patience eyed him, taking in the appealing way his hair had tousled underneath his hat. He set said garment aside for a moment and stepped closer.

"Well?"

"I am not sure your sister to be will be happy with you calling it malarkey."

"Do not change the subject. Will you stay a little longer?"

The warm, earnest look in his eyes had her practically unravelling. Had she not been leaning against one of the wooden struts inside the barn she might have collapsed altogether. It would be far too easy and appealing to believe Nate truly wanted her, but if he did not, what was this game?

"I should return home."

"Perhaps."

"I mean, I *really* ought to return home."

"Maybe."

"Nate, I must."

"Why? Your brother knows you are here, with your fiancé. As long as I have you returned by nightfall there is nothing that can be said."

"Yes, but we both know you are not really my fiancé."

"Until you break it off with me, you are."

She studied his resolute expression and huffed. "This is—"

A blur of white cut her off. The sheep rushed in front of her. Nate held up his hands. "Sheep, behave," he commanded.

The animal ignored him and went barreling into him, forcing him to take a step back. All would have been well had the back of his legs not connected with the trough behind him. The sheep backed off only briefly before giving Nate one more nudge, as if intending to seal her master's fate.

It seemed to happen slowly. There were flailing arms, a slight look of panic which Patience rather enjoyed considering she had never seen the man look panicked in his life. He toppled backward and water splashed about him. The trough rocked slightly but did not tip.

Patience stared and took in the aftermath of the sheep's eager behavior. The creature did several loops of the trough as if inspecting the result. Nate sat, his legs hanging over the side of the trough. His shirt clung to his skin, soaked through. Water trickled down his face and a tinge of furious red haunted his cheeks and forehead.

Patience pressed her lips together but it was no good. A burst of laughter escaped her. Then another. Then more when Nate tried to ease himself out of the trough only to fall back down and create another wave of water. Tears streamed down the side of her face and she clutched her stomach.

"God. Damn. Sheep," Nate muttered.

"Oh dear," she gasped. "You should see..." She tried to suck in a breath to control the laughter. "It really is just so very amusing." Her shoulders shook as another torrent of laughter overtook her.

"Do not just stand there. Help me up," Nate demanded, holding out a hand.

Still giggling, Patience took his hand and braced herself to help pull him up. As soon as his fingers had sealed over hers, she realized her mistake. He gave one brief, hard tug.

The ground went from under her feet. A shock of cold water touched her skin. She toppled completely in, landing atop him. His eyes were crinkled with mirth.

She gave him a splash and laughed. "Now, how am I meant to return home?"

"Precisely."

"Did you plan this?"

An eyebrow lifted. "Plan to have that blasted sheep push me into a trough? Unlikely." He gave her a little shove and inched her forward out of the trough. "Come on, let us get out of here before we catch a chill."

She put her hands onto the edge of the metal and with one rather ungentlemanly push to her rear, she was out. Turning, she offered her hand to Nate.

"You had better not pull me in again."

He lifted a hand. "I swear it."

She helped him up and water sluiced off him. He shoved a hand through his hair, turning the tousled waves curlier. Patience grinned.

"I cannot tell if your sheep loves you or hates you."

He returned the grin. "Sometimes I cannot either."

When her gaze fell from his smile, the air in her lungs froze. It was not the first time she had seen his body but there was something different about it in a wet shirt. The way the cotton clung and molded to him had her stumbling for words, or actions. All she could do was stare.

She tried like the devil to swallow the knot in her throat but it would not budge. When she finally managed to tear her gaze upward, she realized he had not even noticed her paralysis. He had been too busy staring as well. She now understood that if she looked at her own shirt, there would be a similar image except he would be able to see her breasts and probably the indent of her waist.

It hit her hard. This was it. This was what it felt like to be a powerful, strong woman, able to command a man to do her bidding. Except, of course, now she had him under her command, she was not at all sure what to do with him.

His gaze lifted to hers and the power shifted. Now it was equal, weighted between them and drawing them together. She no longer questioned what to do.

They collided at the same time, their wet shirts sticking to one another. His body was warm beneath the cold cotton. Warm and hard, and impossible to resist.

His hand cupped her neck, the pressure strong and unrelenting. There would be no escaping him. Not that she wanted to. She let her gaze fall briefly to his lips before gazing into his eyes. Any breath she had left in her body vanished in a puff of smoke.

Patience looped her hands around his neck.

"Christ, what are you doing to me?" he asked, the words gruff and raw.

She had no time to answer. Even if she did, she would not know how to respond. His lips came down upon her slightly parted ones. Hot, demanding, passionate. Her eyelids fluttered closed of their own accord and she was lost. Lost to the feel of his body against hers, lost to the way his hands held her close, treasured her, made her feel desirable and beautiful.

His tongue touched hers and she trembled. Her bones had turned to liquid and were it not for his embrace, she would be puddled on the floor like melted ice.

Nate rocked his hips into hers. Any thoughts of her wet shirt, or even his, were long gone. Heat flared through her as though she were standing next to a raging fire. He broke away briefly— long enough to pepper kisses down her neck and nibble her jawline. He left her wanting, panting and needy. His words echoed in her mind. *What are you doing to me? What are you doing to me?*

What was he doing to her, more like? Every idea of common sense had fled her. The only thoughts that existed were *More!* and *Oh yes, there!* and *More, more, more!* Once his hands began moving up and down her back, she began to move with him, pressing herself into him. An ache that only seemed to worsen gathered between her thighs.

She groaned. He kissed her harder. Patience responded, sweeping her tongue into his mouth. A wild sound tore from Nate and he gripped her hips tight. As he did so, she stumbled back. They toppled together onto the straw. Nate barely gave her a moment to catch her breath. Cushioned by the straw, she accepted the onslaught of his fiery kisses, a moan escaping her as his body covered hers.

"What. Do. You. Do. To. Me?" he asked between kisses once more.

She understood it now. She aroused him. Somehow, she—the eccentric girl who wore breeches and hunted with her brothers and did not know how to embroider—aroused this man. That's what she did to him. And he did the same to her. Every inch of her was alight, desperate for his touch, his kiss.

That same fire burned inside her, making her feel full and wonderful. Her heart stretched with each peppered kiss against her skin. She eyed the beams above for a moment to try to get herself centered and ensure this was really happening. And it was.

Nathaniel Kingsley had his mouth upon her neck, his hand on one breast. He moved atop her, rubbing against her in a way that mimicked everything she wanted from him. She did not even have to cast her mind back to know she had never felt this before. The desperation building inside should have been terrifying but it wasn't, not when she was sharing it with Nate.

He plucked a button, opening her shirt a fraction. Hot breath whispered over the curve of her breasts. She could feel them rising and falling against her undergarments. Nate eased back just enough to eye her.

She could imagine the picture she made—sprawled on the straw, her hair wild, her shirt open. She could imagine it and she could see herself in his eyes. She, Patience Grey, was beautiful, and powerful, and sensual. She with her boyish waist and short legs, was enchanting even.

From the look in Nate's eyes she was right. Goodness, so this is what it felt like to be a beautiful woman? She was almost heady from the experience.

"Patience, Patience, Patience," he murmured, returning to cover her body with his. His lips tickled across the tops of her breasts, making her nipples ache and throb.

She arched instinctively into him and he hooked a hand beneath her back.

"Beautiful Patience," he whispered and the words danced a pattern of breath across her skin. "Beautiful, beautiful Patience. Christ, no wonder I never stood a chance."

"What...what do you mean?" she managed to croak.

She regretted the words when he moved up onto his elbow to look down at her. However, she could not resist lifting a palm to touch his cheek and push aside a strand of hair that had dropped across his forehead. To touch him so freely left her feeling tingly inside.

"You're bewitching, Patience."

"You had better not say that in public. It would not be a stretch of the imagination for people to think me a real witch."

He chuckled. "Perhaps you are." Nate dropped a kiss on her lips and rose back up. "Will you call it off?"

A wash of coldness tumbled over her as though she had been dunked in the trough once more. "You must," she insisted.

"I will not."

"Nor will I."

He grinned. It was the usual charming, heart-wrenching grin that he often threw her way yet there was something different to it. As though he had not summoned it to charm her but he genuinely could not keep it from spreading across his lips.

"Then it looks as though we are getting married."

Staring at him, she frowned. He said the words so matter-of-factly, as if he were talking of them going for a stroll or having dinner. As if it would not change both their lives irrevocably.

"We do not have to if you simply stop being stubborn and call it off."

He gave a shrug. "I will not call it off. You will not call it off. I see no other way to end this other than us getting married."

She blinked several times as she searched her mind for a response. "But...but...why would you not break it off?" It made no sense. She had been certain he would do it eventually, at least before the banns were read. There was no chance Nate would let this farce continue. Once he was back in society—or what little society there was in Penshallow—he would forget about her and be more than happy to say he had made a mistake and he wished to move on.

"Would us marrying be so terrible?"

Suddenly his proximity was too much. He took her mind and whirled it around, made her unable to think. She wriggled to get free from him and he shrugged and eased away. Patience drew her legs up and looped her arms around them.

"You cannot possibly want me for your wife?"

"Why ever not?"

"Because...because I am not wifely material."

He ran his gaze over her, reminding her of her disheveled state. She clutched her blouse together and stood. He followed suit which made her wish she had stayed sitting. Now he had the advantage of height and handsomeness. His shirt remained plastered to him so she could not forget the strength and beauty of that body that had been pressed against her.

"Patience, you are more than wifely material. You are courageous, intelligent, funny, and sensual."

Sensual. That was a word she had never heard describe her. Then again, she was not sure she had heard any of the others either. Eccentric, yes. Strange, certainly. Stubborn and aggravating too. But none of those.

She eyed him, hunting for some sign of a lie or ulterior motive behind the flattery. She could find none.

Nate extended his hand. "Come, I shall find you a dry shirt. No doubt it shall be too big for you but hopefully none shall notice once you have your riding jacket back on."

Patience swallowed against the dryness in her mouth and nodded. He could not truly want her, could he? Yet, as unconvinced as she was, she took his hand and allowed him to lead her into the house.

Any relief Nate felt at Patience agreeing to remain vanished when Red greeted him at the house with a grim expression. His brother's expression barely flickered at their damp state.

"You have a visitor. Patience's brother Jacob. I have put him in the blue drawing room."

Patience threw a puzzled glance his way but before she could question her brother's arrival, Hannah scurried in. Red's pretty fiancé clapped a hand over her mouth. "What happened to you two? It did not rain today, did it?" She paused when she spotted Patience's embarrassed expression. "Well, these things happen. Believe me, I should know."

A spark of amusement danced between Red and Hannah. Nate had not been appraised of everything that had happened during their time together only weeks before but Red had confessed Hannah had ended up soaked to the skin at one point and was forced to strip to her chemise. It had been that moment that had ruined him forever, his brother confessed.

"Come with me and I shall find you a change of clothes." Hannah held out her hand expectantly.

Patience gave Nate a helpless look and took Hannah's hand. Once they were out of earshot, he leaned into Red. "I can assume this is not a friendly visit, can I not?"

His brother shrugged. "I cannot say but Jacob did not look best pleased."

"Well, best get this over and done with."

He strode to the blue drawing room and pushed open the door. Nate briefly considered sitting but decided against it. If this were taking place in a bar or a darkened alleyway, he would be preparing himself for a fight. Jacob eyed him, arms folded.

Nate forwent any formal greetings. He knew what this was about. "I take it Pauline is deposited safely."

"She is."

"The leg causing you any trouble?"

Jacob's jaw flexed.

"Come on, Jacob, out with it."

Jacob took several steps forward and thrust a finger in his face. "You need to call this off with Patience. You know this was never meant to turn into a real damned marriage."

Nate cocked his head. "Harry seems happy with the match."

"Harry thought she'd never find anyone. He'd be happy if she married a pig-farmer. He seems willing to ignore your past...behavior."

"And what sort of behavior is that?" Nate crossed his arms and lifted his chin.

"The flirting, the tupping, hell, even the smuggling. My sister deserves better."

Nate nodded slowly. "I see. So I was good enough to ask for help. Good enough to aid you in the past, even, but not good enough for your sister."

"You will call this off, Nate," Jacob demanded. "Call this off or I'll tell her."

"I cannot."

Jacob peered at him. "Why not?"

"I love her," he said simply.

Patience's brother stared at him for several moments. "How is it you have gone from begging me to save you from my sister to falling in love with her?"

Nate released a quick laugh. "I was not begging you to save me from her. I was begging you to save her from herself. If you did not arrive when you did, I may not have been able to protect her."

"From yourself you mean?"

Jacob's hand curled around his neck in moments. Finger pressed deep into his skin, making his face hot and his neck hurt. Nate held up his hands. He would not hurt Patience's brother nor would he fight an injured man.

"I love her, Jacob," he repeated, the words strangled.

"You were going to tup her. Had I not interfered, you would have taken her to bed, that's what you're saying, is it not? All this talk in your letter of her being too wild, too dangerous for the mission, was nonsense."

Nate would have laughed again if he could have, but the pressure on his neck remained and was beginning to send his vision a little blurry. "Well, she is wild."

"Damn it, Nate. I expected better from you." Jacob released him suddenly and thrust him back.

Nate took the moment to draw in a breath and adjust his cravat. "I love your sister. I mean that. Hell, I probably loved her even when I wrote to you. But I didn't know that then. All I knew was that I needed to protect her. I did not trust her not to make rash decisions."

Jacob curled a fist and Nate lifted both hands in a placating move.

"And not about me, I swear it."

Nate inwardly cursed himself for his cowardly move. He should have talked her out of going with Pauline but the truth was, he was terrified she'd go and then what? He'd be left without her.

Damn. Even then he'd been in love with her. He just had not realized it.

"You're a damned animal, Nate," Jacob spat. "How am I to believe you feel differently about my sister to any other woman you've bedded?"

Nate lifted a brow. "You're hardly an innocent."

"This is my sister we are speaking of," Jacob snapped. "I don't give a damn what my past is. The only one that matters is yours."

Nodding, Nate sighed. "I know." He pushed a hand through his hair. "I know. I have been no angel. Heck, I've been worse than that. But I want to marry Patience, and I want to make this a good marriage. I want to devote every waking hour to her." He laughed at himself. "I want that woman more than I've ever wanted anything and I would never, never hurt her. I swear to you, all I want to do is make her happy."

Jacob turned away briefly and paced past the fireplace then back again. "That better be true. You have always been one for the ladies but you were never a liar. I hope that has not changed."

"I swear it."

"Well, then, I suppose..." Jacob drew in a breath and exhaled it slowly. "I suppose you have my blessing." He held out a hand.

A door slammed before Nate could shake it. He turned to see the drawing room door ajar and his gaze connected with Hannah's. He pushed open the door. "Was that Patience?"

Hannah nodded. "I am sorry, Nate. She overheard your conversation. I could not draw her away."

He dashed past her into the secondary drawing room and glanced out of the window. Sure enough, Patience was already mounting her horse. By the time he caught up with her, she would be long gone.

"Where will she be going?" he demanded of Jacob.

Her brother shrugged.

"I need my horse."

Jacob put a hand to his shoulder. "If I were you, let her be. You know what her temper is like. Give her a while then go to her. Tell her everything you told me. If that does not work, then I do not know what will."

Nate pressed his palms against the windowsill and watched her set off at a gallop. His heart pounded so hard in his chest he feared he'd crack a rib. Damn him. Damn his idiocy. Damn him for not understanding sooner how he felt about her. Why had he not been honest? Damn, damn, damn.

Chapter Twenty-Three

Great amber and pink streaks lit the sky, tearing the way across it as though the sky had been sliced by a sword multiple times. The sun lingered on the horizon, not quite ready to give up for the day.

Patience had, however. She had surrendered. She had waved the white flag. Rolled over and played dead. No more of this charade, she told herself.

Not even the rhythmic pounding of her horse's hooves beneath her could soothe away the angry ache throbbing in her heart. She had never felt the likes of it before and she never wanted it again. No wonder she had spent her life avoiding men and romantic feelings. They were simply horrible.

She swiped a tear that rolled traitorously down her cheek and sniffed hard. Unfortunately more followed and by the time she reached home, her cheeks were damp and her eyes sore.

The horse insisted on giving her a quick nuzzle as Patience stowed the gelding in the stable. Apparently the animal knew well how Patience was feeling. Though she did not dare remain with her too long or else the simple affection from the mount would likely have her crumbling to the floor.

To think she nearly—No, she would not say it to herself. Patience stomped from the stable and made her way around the back of the house. Lamps were lit in the drawing room and upstairs so her mother or brother were in. She could not face them with a red nose and likely swollen eyes so she opted for sitting in the gazebo in the garden.

Why had she ever trusted that man? She tore off a leaf from a nearby plant and shredded it into tiny pieces before starting on another poor, defenseless leaf. Why had she ever let herself fall under his spell? These past weeks had been confusing and...and ridiculous. She had not known whether she was coming or going.

But now she knew. She was going. Running far away from Nathaniel Kingsley, the man who did not trust her to do her job. First, she would call off the engagement. She would tell Harry that he was a cad. A man who could not be trusted. Harry might still be disappointed but he would not blame her if he thought Nate was a man of bad character. Then she would go to her cousins' in Devon. Stay there for a few months perhaps. Wait for the gossip to vanish.

And when she returned she would avoid looking that man in the eyes ever again.

A great, ugly sob escaped her. Even as she tried to keep it in. The sound was so hideous that another followed it. Then another. She was not sure if she was crying because she hated that she was crying or because she loathed the thought of never seeing Nate again.

Fool that she was.

That man did not deserve her tears. She flung a half-shredded leaf away and it fluttered onto her lap. She eyed the disobedient leaf and brushed it off her legs. Nate deserved nothing. He had toyed with her, perhaps using her as a momentary distraction. He had used her ill indeed. If anyone understood how much that mission had meant to her, it was Nate. All those quiet evenings spent spilling out secrets she had never admitted to anyone...

A crazed laugh bubbled from her. How foolish she must have sounded. How much he must have laughed. Poor little Patience Grey. No one to talk to but a rogue with no morals.

"What the devil was that noise?"

Patience twisted her head to view Harry heading down the garden path. He carried a candle, much to her regret. Perhaps she would have escaped his sympathy had he not been able to see her face.

She sniffed and shrugged. "Cat perhaps."

He smiled and came to sit by her. "Or a wailing woman."

"Strange. I have seen no wailing women."

Harry set the candleholder on the alcove in the gazebo and twisted to eye her. "I think I have."

A hand reached up to brush her cheek and that did it. She felt herself crumble in two. Harry opened his arms and drew her into them. The shock of the contact made the tears come harder and faster. She could not recall the last time her brother had embraced her. When she was five perhaps and had skinned her knee, or maybe when she fell from a tree at the age of seven.

He brushed her hair with a palm and made soothing noises. She could not be sure what they were because the tears still came. After a while, she could not be sure what she was crying for. The loss of a silly dream perhaps. The idea that maybe, just maybe, someone like Nate could care for her. She imagined some of the tears were for her brother and his care of her. How he had looked after her since she was a young girl and all she longed to do was make him proud—yet she had failed.

Thanks to Nate, she thought bitterly.

When her head began to hurt and her throat grew dry, the tears slowed. Harry did not push her away but let her remain against his chest until her breathing steadied. Finally, she eased herself up and swiped her hot, sticky face with a hand.

Harry offered her a handkerchief and she gave an unladylike blow.

"Better?" he asked.

"I think so." Her voice sounded raw and hollow.

Lifting her head, she gazed out at the garden. The sun had vanished entirely, cloaking it in a black, unrelenting blanket. Clouds hid the stars from view and all that could be seen was that which was lit by the candle.

"Would you like to tell me what that was about?"

Drawing in a long, long breath, she twisted to eye Harry. "I have disappointed you again."

"How so?"

She licked her dry lips. "I failed Jacob's mission."

He scowled. "You found the information. How is that failure?"

"I did not finish it. Jacob did."

"From what I hear, you did all the work. Jacob was merely the messenger. But why should any of that matter to me?"

"Because...because..." She sighed and let her shoulders slump. "Because you are proud of Jacob and George and Edward. They are all serving their country. I just wanted to do the same."

Harry shook his head and laughed a little. "Patience, you have more than made me proud. You always did. Who else could claim to have such a headstrong sister that they need not worry about her falling into the arms of some rogue? Who could say with confidence that their sister could likely take on twenty men twice her size and come away without a scratch? You are without a doubt the strongest and fiercest sister a man could ask for and I am lucky to have you. I have never needed to escort you about the country and search out a boring husband to ensure you settled and were not taken advantage of. I count myself a lucky man."

She absorbed the words but there were so many, it was hard to take them all in. So Harry was proud of her after all then?

"But I do not think you are crying because you supposedly failed. After all, you have been home some time since the mission and you were not crying before."

She squeezed the handkerchief hard between her hands, as though she could crush away the memory of her humiliation. Patience lifted her chin and met her brother's concerned gaze. If she had known how proud of her he was, would she have pushed herself as hard throughout her life? Could she have ignored what she had heard from her father all those years ago before his death? Did she even regret that she had been so competitive? Perhaps.

But perhaps not. After all, she had but only one regret—and that was ever considering giving her heart to Nate.

"I-I have broken off the engagement with Nathaniel Kingsley."

"Ah."

"You are disappointed," she stated, turning her gaze to her lap.

"In him, yes, if it turns out he was not as in love with you as I thought."

She snapped her gaze to his. "You think he was in love with me?"

"Did he never tell you that?"

"Well, I..." No, he had not. But he had told Jacob. He had said many lovely things to her brother that he had yet to say to her. However, that did not excuse his behavior did it? If he truly cared for her, he would not have ruined things for her. The chances were she would never have really gone with Pauline but he stole that choice from her. "Not as such," she finished softly.

"But he does love you?"

Patience lifted a shoulder. "I think so, but..."

"Do you love him?"

"Yes."

The word came out without thought, without it even echoing in her head. Yes, she loved him. She had likely loved him for some time now. Since their first nights alone, maybe. It was hard to tell. It had been sneaking up on her, working its way into her very bones.

Love.

It now pounded in her heart with every beat. *Love, love, love.* But did she want to love a man that would so disregard her needs, even if he did seem to think he was somehow saving her from herself?

"Patience, Nathaniel Kingsley is everything a brother could want for a sister—in rank and wealth. However, his character leaves something to be desired. That said, the very obvious love he had for you from the moment I saw him persuaded me that if you did indeed love him, I should give you my blessing."

"His character..." She drew in a breath. "His character is..." She smiled. "Nathaniel Kingsley is a rogue. He is a flirt. He's the most infuriating, pig-headed, annoying man I have ever met. But I was wrong about him for the most part. He is loyal and trustworthy. He has done more for this country than most people will ever understand, at great peril."

Harry frowned but let her continue.

The soft smile refused to abate. "He is not so very bad, I suppose."

Harry chuckled. "If he is not so very bad, why are you breaking off the engagement?"

She shook her head slowly. "I am not sure. I do not know if the things that I thought were important are now."

Her brother squeezed her hand. "Let me be the older, wiser brother for but a moment. I am no expert in love—God knows I have yet to find my match—but there are few men who could keep up with you, Patience. I believe Nate is one of them. If he has your best interests at heart, then whatever had happened to make you think badly of him, I suggest you at least speak with him about it. You do have a tendency to leap without thinking. Do not ruin a chance at love."

Patience peered at her brother. "When did you become so wise?"

"The war," he said grimly, "makes one grow up fast. Besides, raising three brothers and a sister does tend to make one mature rather swiftly."

"We are lucky to have you."

"And I you. Now, what are you going to do about this chap of yours?"

Patience smiled. She had an idea.

Chapter Twenty-Four

Nate eyed the bed with distaste. It did not matter how late it was, how could he possibly sleep? He tugged off his cravat in a half-hearted attempt to ready for bed and set down his cufflinks on the mahogany armoire. Red had little sympathy for him and had ordered him off to bed so he and Hannah did not have to look at his miserable face any longer. It was all very well for them, *they* had each other. What did he have?

A sort of fiancée, who was not really his fiancée, but one whom everyone thought was his fiancée, who he really did wish to become his fiancée but likely never would now.

Anyway, he did not much wish to be around those two. With the wedding mere weeks away, their obvious love for one another was becoming harder to stomach. Particularly when he was well-aware he had ruined everything.

Tomorrow. He would go and talk to Patience tomorrow. Or more likely get an earful from her. Either way, he'd face his fate, tell her the truth behind his actions and grovel on his knees if he had to. Apparently when it came to Patience he was not beyond that. His letter to Jacob had been rash and foolish but after he thought he was going to lose her to some exotic, dangerous country, he had decided he had to stop her for her own good.

Look where that had brought him.

Down to his knees if needs be, it seemed.

What an arrogant fool he was. He slipped off his waistcoat and unbuttoned his shirt. Moving over to the washbasin, he dunked his hands in the cold water and bent to splash it across his face. Nate straightened, pushed damp fingers through his hair and let out the hundredth sigh of that night.

Maybe he should have gone after her. He did not know. Of course Patience would be furious but what were the chances of her calming down by the morning? He'd almost rather have faced her straight away than let her stew away, getting angrier by the moment and concocting all sorts of revenge.

He had acquiesced to Jacob because he was her brother. He knew her better. Except, Nate was not so sure now. Patience had never confided with any of her brothers about how she felt, how she longed so badly to make them proud. Only he knew that.

The more he thought about it, the more he grew convinced that he knew her better than them all.

Glancing at the clock, he debated it. If he turned up now and Harry was aware Nate had upset Patience, he might end up called out for a duel or at least end up with a door slammed in his face. He probably deserved to be called out. He had not been honest with Patience and for that he had paid dearly.

But damn it, he needed to see her. No other woman had ever tangled him up in knots so. No one had been able to cause him such anguish. That was simply because no other woman was like Patience.

His hand hovered over his jacket. To go or not to go. Before he could make the decision, there was a rattle at the window. He scowled and peered at it. There was no rain tonight nor wind. Unless a great tree had suddenly sprouted overnight, there was nothing that could make such a noise.

The rattle—that was more like a tap when he thought about it—happened again. He strode over and slung back the curtains.

He nearly fell over backwards.

"Patience, bloody hell." He yanked at the handle on the window only to find the cold weather had made it seize up. He tried again. "Bloody, goddamn, bloody, idiot woman. What in the hell..." he muttered as he wrangled with the metal latch.

It finally gave way and he tore open the window to haul her in. He yanked her in so fast and hard that they toppled to the floor together. He released an *oof* and found himself momentarily dazed.

Nate blinked several times before focusing his vision on the woman on top of him. Her hair was wild around her shoulders, a golden, frizzy mess that made her face seem petite. She wore a dress. The same god-awful pink one that should have been consigned to a bonfire as soon as it had been designed. The dress was tied around her legs much like the night they had broken into Magnus' house.

That was not the most unusual thing about her, however. No, it was the wide grin on her face that baffled him. Maybe she was considering throwing a punch his way and that was the cause for amusement.

"You're a damned foolish woman," he said, grabbing her arms and easing her off him. "If you wanted to shout at me, you could have come through the front door.

He stood and slammed shut the window. The window shook in protest and he winced. He turned to her and thrust out a finger. "No more climbing damned buildings, do you understand me? No more, little one. You could have killed yourself."

She said nothing, merely held onto that strange smile that only made him madder. What was she thinking, scaling the walls of the hall? His room was a whole level higher than the window at Magnus' house.

"What would I have done had you died?" he continued. "What—"

She grabbed his face in both hands, rose onto tiptoes and flatted her lips to his.

"What would I have done?" he said, the words smothered.

Patience drew back long enough to shush him then kissed him again. The fight vanished. He had no idea why she was kissing him or what the devil was happening, and he did not much care. Let her silence him forever with her kisses. He would die a happy man.

Hands to his shoulders, she coaxed him around so that his back was to the bed. She took a step back and gave him a gentle shove. He fell back onto the bed and pushed himself up onto his elbows to view her.

Ugly pink dress or not, he had never desired anyone with as much intensity as this. From her halo of messy hair to the bunched fabric around her muscled calves, he could not want her more.

Fists on hips, she eyed him, and he had to wonder if this was not part of some plan of revenge. Get him aroused then humiliate him in some way. If so, he would gladly take part. He would do whatever she bid if it gave him a chance to try to explain himself to her.

"Patience, I—"

She came forward and climbed atop him, knees on either side of his legs. The sweet, fresh scent of her clouded about him. He glanced at her cleavage which was directly in his line of sight. Actually, the dress was not so bad after all if he thought about it. The way it cupped her generous breasts while giving him the tiniest hint of flesh was enough to drive a man wild.

"I like this dress," he said, his apology forgotten momentarily.

"You do?" She laughed. "I thought it was hideous."

"Why wear it then?"

"Because, Lord Nathaniel Kingsley, I intend to seduce you." She leaned forward, forcing him to lie back on the bed.

Her hair drifted over him, teasing his skin. Her thighs held him in place while the apex of her thighs pressed hard against his arousal. His eyes near rolled back in his head.

"You're doing a fine job." The words came out strangled. "But why?" he managed to force out as her breath whispered over his lips and across his slightly stubbled chin.

She pressed a kiss to the side of his neck and a tremor of anticipation rioted through him. Then she put her lips to his Adam's apple and down to his collar bone. She came up long enough to remove his glasses and set them aside before continuing this wonderfully torturous pattern of kissing all over his face until she came to his lips.

"I heard what you said." The words were uttered against his cheek.

"I know, and, Patience, you should know that—"

"You love me."

"Well, yes that too."

"Good." She lifted her head to meet his gaze. "I love you too."

Any reply vanished. The bumbling words of apology were gone. A fanfare of triumph sounded in his mind. *Yes, yes, yes.* He had this woman's love. And, apparently, she was not at all angry.

By the time he'd considered summoning more words of apology, she was kissing him again. And rubbing. God almighty, there was rubbing. Her body rocked against his, sending surge after surge of pleasure through him. He drew in a breath and pushed his hands through her hair. Whatever had happened between her finding out about what he had done and now, he hardly cared anymore. All he knew was that Patience loved him and was intent on driving him over the edge. Well, if she was going to push him into the abyss, he was taking her with him.

He kissed her back hard and fast, delving deep and drinking in the taste of her. When he broke away briefly to draw in a breath, he saw flushed cheeks and glistening skin.

"Where did you learn to seduce?" he asked. Half of him was jesting but the other had him worrying she had been putting her skills to practice elsewhere.

"From you."

"From me?"

She nodded and tucked her bottom lip under her teeth. A smile curved her lips. "You taught me all I know about being a woman."

He lifted his brows. "Well, that was clever of me."

Patience chuckled. "Do you not see? All those compliments, all that flirtation. All those roguish comments and those kisses and touches, they...well, they made me understand."

"Understand what?"

"That there is no shame in wearing a dress and being feminine. That there is nothing weak in being womanly. That, essentially, it can be quite a powerful experience. You taught me that."

He eyed this brave, bold woman in front of him with a smile. "And here I thought you knew everything."

"Almost everything," she conceded.

"I can teach you more."

"Then do," she begged. "Then do."

Nate needed no more coercion. Not that he ever needed any in the first place. He rolled her onto her back. Peppering kisses over her neck and the rise of her breasts, he began to untangle the dress from around her legs. He worked her stockings down and found her mouth with his. She writhed underneath him, moving her body like a wave on the ocean, beckoning him to his doom.

Well, doomed man that he was, he was more than happy to sink with this ship. Once he had worked off her gown and discovered, much to his delight that only a slip remained underneath, he set to work on drowning himself in her. He pushed up the cotton to eye the soft flesh of her thighs. He kissed and bit at the inside of them while urging the chemise higher.

Nate set a light kiss to her slightly rounded belly then up, and up. "Christ almighty." He damned well nearly spilled in his breeches then and there. The woman had the most spectacular breasts a man had ever set eyes on.

When her breasts were fully revealed and her chemise had been cast aside, he continued kissing his way along her trembling body. Her fingernails ran tracks over his skin, leaving trails of tingling sensation all over him. His cock strained against the confines of his clothes.

He gave her a firm kiss and stood. For the most part it was to remove his clothing, but it also gave him the added advantage of admiring her spread across his bed. Her arms were slightly browner than the rest of her and a tiny 'v' of color where her shirt always remained open led his eye down to her breasts. Her nipples were pink and pale, and just perfect for tasting.

A blush of color ran across her chest and up into her face. "What are you doing?"

He fought with the buttons of his shirt. "Undressing." He frowned at the buttons that seemed to have become the smallest buttons in the world and were completely impossible to hold onto. "Trying to."

She moved to sit up but he motioned her down. "Stay. I want to admire you. Do not move a muscle."

He saw her throat work but she did as he bid and remained utterly still, her eyes steadily widening as he finally mastered buttons and revealed his chest then stripped to his skin. She swallowed again.

"I will not hurt you," he promised, placing his body over hers. "I know."

Though the temptation to bury himself deep inside her was fierce, he did not give in. Patience's pleasure and comfort would be his first thought. His cock touched her damp quim and he groaned. She let out a hiss and shuddered. He grinned to himself as he buried his face into the crook of her neck and nibbled at the sensitive skin there.

He moved again, touching his arousal to her folds and that same shudder repeated itself. Shifting his hips, he moved slightly harder, each time brushing his cock up and down her sensitive spot. Her nails dug into his shoulders.

If he focused hard, he could forget the pleasure it brought him. He forced himself to think only of her slightly whimpering noises and the subtle movements of her body. With each gentle, rubbing thrust, her body grew more limp, more pliable. The whimpers turned into cries. He picked up the pace until she stiffened and her nails bit into his skin in a far too pleasurable way. His name spilled from her lips in a breathy cry and she wilted.

Nate moved back to view her and pushed her hair from her dampened face. "You are not the only one who can seduce," he said with a grin.

"No," she agreed, drawing in a long, shuddering breath. "I am not."

He eased up her leg and opened her to him. With one finger, he tested her, finding her wet and ready. He placed in another finger, then another. Her eyes widened but there was no pain there.

Lowering himself down onto her, he urged her legs over his hips and kissed her hard before moving back. He wanted to see her expression for many reasons. Firstly, to ensure he did not hurt her but secondly so he could never forget the time he made Patience his.

He inched in cautiously, jaw clenched as the tightness closed in around him. The desire to close his eyes warred with the need to see her. He eased forward again, surely moving at the slowest pace a man had ever moved. His muscles strained with restraint.

Deeper again. Deeper, deeper. Her eyes were wide, her mouth was open in an 'o' shape. Hair splayed over his bedsheets, her hands now digging into his rear, she was the picture of seduction. How could any man resist?

He moved one more time and waited. In those several heartbeats, he absorbed the sensation of being joined with the woman he loved. Hand on heart, it was nothing like he had ever experienced before.

"Going to marry you," he murmured before easing back and sliding in again.

She moaned. "Yes."

"You wish to marry me?"

"Yes," she repeated, her lids fluttering as he picked up the pace. "Yes, yes, yes."

Nate would have to ask her again when he was not buried deep inside of her to be certain but for now he would take that as a yes.

The pleasure built as he kissed her deep, their tongues tangling. As Patience began to understand the rhythm, she moved her hips with him, bringing more ecstasy than he thought possible. Her body began to quiver and tighten around him, and he gritted his teeth to keep control.

Her peak came slowly, rolling over them both in subtle waves. She uttered another soft "Yes" and her body spasmed one last time. He gave himself up to her then, closing his eyes and groaning loudly as he spilled into her in one gut-wrenching orgasm.

Pushing up onto his elbows, he stared down at the woman who had changed his life irrevocably and realized he had no regrets. He was always looking for his next adventure, after all, and it seemed Patience would be that—and he had no doubt she would keep him on his toes for the rest of his life.

"I never meant to hurt you," he said quickly.

"You did not. That was wonderful." She smoothed a palm over his cheek and he nearly forgot what he wanted to say.

"No, with regards to telling Jacob he needed to come and help."

"I know."

"Do you? Do you understand how insane you made me? I could hardly think straight. I was scared, little one. Scared of the lengths you would go to and scared you would leave me."

"You? Scared? Surely not."

He nodded. Admitting that one was scared should not have felt like a good thing and yet it did. The burden had fallen from his shoulders and left him feeling weightless.

"You are an amazing woman. How could I ever hope to keep you happy?"

"More moments like this would be nice," she said with a grin.

"Saucy wench," he teased.

"I was angry," she admitted. "You know why."

"I do."

"But I realized I had been chasing the wrong things for the wrong reasons. And that I had to chase the things I wanted. Namely, you."

If he grinned any harder, he would break his face. So he kissed her forehead and eased off her so he could wrap her in his arms. "Well, you have no need to chase me any longer. I am yours. For better or for worse."

Epilogue

"Do not be jealous, Red."

Nate's brother narrowed his gaze at him. "I am not jealous."

"Could have fooled me." Nate pointed to his cravat. "Does this look right to you? Hamilton could not seem to get it right this morning."

"Your valet is one of the best there is. It looks fine."

Nate peered into the full-length mirror and scowled. He had to look perfect for Patience, especially after all the fuss there had been over The Dress. It would be the only time he would ever see Patience actually interested in a gown and he would not ruin things for her by looking less than flawless.

"What is the time?" Nate demanded.

Red pulled out his pocket watch. "Time to leave. Your fiancé should be at the church soon."

Nate nodded, drew in a breath and straightened his waistcoat once more. There was little he could do now. If he tweaked or toyed with his finery any longer they would be late to the church and Patience would string him up for making her wait.

He glanced at his brother's frown. "Do stop scowling. You are meant to be the proud brother."

"I am not." Red attempted to smile and it was thoroughly disconcerting.

"Your wedding is a mere week away. It will be your turn soon."

Red shook his head and genuinely smiled this time. "It has been too damned long."

"I knew you were jealous."

"Well, some of us have to do things properly, unfortunately."

"Whereas I am the scandalous younger brother who swept a woman off her feet and now must make things right by marrying her." He grinned.

"Indeed." His brother lifted a brow. "But I am glad you are making things right. You would have been damned miserable had you not persuaded Patience to marry you."

Nate lifted a chin. "I like to think she would have been miserable without me too."

"If you say so," Red said dryly. "Come let us not keep your bride waiting."

Nate and his brother headed out to the carriage. Hannah waited for them inside, having announced they needed some time alone together. Perhaps she expected Red to give him some words of wisdom but Nate needed none. He knew full well what he needed to do with Patience. Love her, treasure her, worship the damned ground she walked on. A woman like her made that easy enough because, quite frankly, it was no less than what she deserved.

Knight and Drake were also huddled into the carriage. It was odd to see Knight squashed into a formal waistcoat and jacket. He half expected the gold buttons to pop off at any moment as the carriage set off.

They mostly remained silent on the journey to the church. Nate tried not to fidget but it was hard to remain still when he considered how close he was to marrying Patience. They had arranged a quick wedding with a license from the bishop to avoid having to read the banns. Most of the village had been merrily gossiping about them anyway so it was no big scandal. As far as he was concerned, he could not wait to make her officially his wife. He understood his brother's frustration at having to wait so long to wed Hannah.

Many of the villagers were gathered outside the church when they arrived. Nate shook many hands and uttered a few *thank yous* as men and women wished him well. He paused as he spotted a familiar face. The woman, her face mostly hidden under a huge hat, gave him a slow smile.

"I would have thought you had left the country by now."

Pauline's smile expanded. "Soon," she said.

"Managed to give the government men a slip then?"

"Of course."

"I wish you well."

"As do I. I will not stay but be sure to tell Patience that I hope she embraces her next adventure. And I hope she has flung away that awful pink dress."

Nate laughed and recalled the last time she had worn the hideous garment. Truth be told, he had quite an affection for it now. He should put it in a frame or have it locked in a treasure box.

"*Au revoir*, Nathaniel." Pauline twisted into the crowd and vanished. Nate shook his head at the brief encounter. He had a suspicion Pauline would have no problems settling wherever she went and likely finding some generous donor to provide her with all that she needed.

Patience did not leave him waiting too long. When the church doors opened, his heart nearly leapt out of his throat and flopped onto the aisle. Not from nerves, however. He had simply never seen anything quite like it. The Dress was well worth all the fuss it seemed. White lace and delicate embroidery with a matching bonnet had turned his Patience into quite the site to behold.

As she beamed at him, he could feel a ridiculous grin taking hold and there was little he could do about it. What made his smile increase was the sight of the sheep, walking on a lead next to Patience, flowers twined around the leather.

She came to his side and handed the sheep over to her brother Jacob, and they faced the vicar while everyone settled into the pews. He leaned into Patience.

"The Dress is wonderful. You look spectacular."

"Thank you." A tinge of color appeared on her cheeks.

"I hope this does not mean this is the end of the breeches."

"Never," she promised.

Something nudged the back of his legs and urged him closer to Patience. Nate turned to find the sheep backing up and preparing for another shove. Jacob gave him an apologetic look and tried to rein the animal back in.

"I think the sheep wants us to get on with it."

Patience nodded. "I think she might be right." He leaned down to kiss her and the soft touch of her lips almost made him forget they had an audience of just under one hundred. The vicar coughed and Nate straightened.

"May I?" the vicar asked.

Nate chuckled. "Please do." He had never been more ready for his next adventure.

THE END

Author's Note

Pauline Fourès did exist. She was Napoleon's mistress and her early history in this story is correct. However, I took a few liberties and brought her to England. In reality, she divorced her horrible husband whilst they were stationed in Egypt where divorce was relatively easy. She remained Napoleon's mistress for some two months more until he went to Syria and then France. Very simply, Napoleon eventually lost interest—or was perhaps wary of creating scandal when he became First Consul—and refused to see her when she returned to France. He gifted her a house near Paris and money. She married not long after.

Her later history is what interested me most in her. She was a painter, a harp player, wrote two novels, and moved to Brazil to sell exotic wood to France with a new husband. She lived a long—and hopefully happy—life finally returning to Paris to live in an apartment surrounded by monkeys.

Made in the USA
Middletown, DE
09 February 2020